OTHER PEOPLE'S LIVES

JE ROWNEY

LITTLE FOX
PUBLISHING

Also by this author

Psychological Fiction

I Can't Sleep

The Woman in the Woods

Women's Fiction

Charcoal

The Derelict Life of Evangeline Dawson

Ghosted

Starting Out

The On-Call Midwife at Christmas

The Lessons of a Student Midwife Series

Life Lessons

Love Lessons

Lessons Learned

Visit jerowney.com/about-je-rowney for a
FREE book, and to preview and buy my novels.

ISBN: 9781739689902

CHAPTER ONE

Dear Jack,

It's been six months, and I know you may never read my letters. Letters were always my thing anyway, weren't they? I had to stay in touch somehow, while you were out there. You never replied, not even a card on the birthdays you spent all those miles away from me. I knew you'd received them, because you brought them back with you, the envelopes carefully opened with one slice along the top: slit not peeled, never ripped.

Everything you did was always so methodical. Was. I'm using the past tense, but a part of me still believes – still wants to believe – you are out there, somewhere. I want to believe I'll be in the kitchen, emptying my shopping bag, putting away the meals-for-one, sliding the single pint of milk into the refrigerator door, stashing the small loaf that I know I will never get through on my own, and I'll hear you fumbling for your keys on the doorstep outside, just like you always did. You would reach into one pocket, then the other. That oversized coat with the flaps and the faux fur hood had so many hiding places. You wanted to look like an adventurer even in those breaks back home with me.

Your assignment was meant to last six weeks, but here we are, heading into June, and I am alone. At least I hope I'm alone.

It's nothing. It's stress, anxiety, whatever a woman gets when her husband goes missing. I'm writing all the wrong things; I don't blame you. It's not your fault that you're not here. I'm sure I'm worrying about nothing. The morning you left; I was wrong to snap at you. You had enough on your mind with the pressure of the trip and the importance of your study. I was stupid. I know that now. So what if you weren't going to be home for Christmas? Other people have their holidays together, but that doesn't mean we have to. We've never been like everybody else. Other people's lives were never as interesting as ours.

The bottom line is that I want you home. I want to pick up the wet towels you drop on the bathroom floor, rinse the mugs you leave by the side of the sofa, iron your shirts, wake up every morning and kiss you even if you're up at six and I don't have to work until nine. I want the inconveniences of you, and I want the joys of you. I want you here with me. I can't bear the waiting, the endless longing for your return.

I'm going to keep writing these letters. Maybe I'm doing it for you, or maybe this is for me. I need someone to talk to. At least if I write it down, it doesn't feel like I'm talking to myself. That would be one more thing to take to my sessions with Doctor Thacker.

Yes, I've finally done it. I didn't want to, but what else was there to do? I know you would have made me go sooner. If you were here, though, maybe I wouldn't need to go at all. Not that I'm blaming you. None of this is your fault. You are missing and I am missing you. Funny how that works.

Thinking of you always,
Come home.
Soph

CHAPTER TWO

The first half hour of the day is the least interesting. There's always paperwork to read, forms to sign, prep to do for the coming day. Henny does a lot of the groundwork; the documents are usually on the desk next to a fresh cup of tea by eight thirty. She's the most efficient of the assistants, the eldest, but also, undeniably, the most attractive. Perhaps it's her caring, mumsy nature that makes me think of her in that way. She does all those little things without even thinking, or at least she gives the impression they are unconscious, automatic, just part of who she is.

I call her Henny because she's like a mother hen, always clucking around. She wears her greying brown hair up in one of those clips that doesn't quite keep it all together, adding to the messy-feathered effect. She's in and out of the room in a flash, wanting to do her job but not get in the way.

I don't see much of her, but I'm always aware of her presence in the background. She has a kind of sixth sense, like she's there just before she's needed. The other girl, Lola, doesn't have the same experience or intuitive nature. Most days, the two of them cover the office work between them, but Henny has taken to having Fridays off over the past few months. The difference in atmosphere without her is palpable. You could switch Lola out for any run-of-the-mill assistant, and the office would still run, the tea would be made, documents filed, patients welcomed; nothing would change. Henny though, she's part of the essence of the place.

Lola is the chatty type, always the one leaning on the desk, talking to the next patient, client, customer, whatever I'm meant to call them. It's not like she oversteps the mark. I mean, I never hear her talking about any personal details or intimacies. It's always the usual mindless small talk you'd expect in a hairdresser's salon rather than in a psychiatrist's waiting room. When I first met her, I asked her to tone it down, to aim for polite and interested rather than pushy and invasive, and she's tried to find a middle ground since. I have to give her credit for that. She does listen. Henny would rather get her work done, focus on what she is meant to be doing rather than what she wants to do. I think there's something to be said about that. If you're happy in your own existence, perhaps you're not quite as interested in poking your nose into other people's lives. Still, this is a psychiatrist's practice, so other people's lives are de facto open books.

Today is Tuesday, and Tuesday has recently become my favourite day. I spend the first half hour thinking about what's coming. I'm not thinking about the paperwork or the tea. I'm thinking about Sophie. Today, this particular Tuesday, will be Sophie's third appointment. She's been going through the awkward openings phase – the introduction of who she is, why she's been referred to a psychiatrist and what she wants to achieve. You'd think that would be straightforward, that the answer would be that she wants to get better, but better than what? And isn't *better* just a place on a scale? If you start off at rock bottom, then even one step in the right direction could be seen as feeling better.

For the first couple of sessions, she definitely didn't feel better. She felt worse. Opening up, describing the way she had been feeling, trying to explain what had changed, why she might be feeling this way, offloading all of that in two one-hour chunks. It took it out of her. The crux of it is this, though, Sophie Portman thinks that someone is watching her.

It was her opening line. The answer to the routine invitation: *so, tell me why you are here today.*

"I think someone's watching me."

She paused, as if wondering what to say next, while I sat, watching, waiting for her to continue. I wanted the words to come from her mouth without prompting. She must have rehearsed the sentence in her head, built herself up to saying it, because once she had delivered the line, she didn't seem to know what to say next. She was a woman without a plan.

Sophie looked down at her hands, as though her chipped nail varnish was suddenly the most interesting thing in the world, and ran a finger over the tattered remains on the end of her left index finger. Her sleek hair looked perfectly maintained, and she was wearing clothes that perfectly suited her petite, albeit slightly curvy frame, but apparently, she didn't have time for a manicure.

Anyway, I waited. Time passed, time that she was paying for. Eventually, she turned her eyes upward, finally connecting, and began to speak. Slowly, steadily at first, but once she started, the words tumbled in a flurry from her mouth

"I need help. I know I need help. It's stupid. I haven't seen anyone, not really. At least, I don't know. I've seen... I don't know what I've seen. I'm on the street, broad daylight, walking past the post office, wondering whether I have time to pop into the Oxfam shop before my bus comes, nothing unusual, just your normal kind of day, and I don't know, I feel like there's someone behind me. Do you know what I mean? That sensation, like eyes boring into me. I turn around, and... nothing. I'm in my house, standing in the kitchen, making a cup of coffee to have while I settle down and watch another crappy quiz show. I glance up and I'm sure there's someone there, a figure by the tree in my garden. I've already looked away, though. The kettle's boiled and distracted me, and when I look back, there's no one there. It was a shadow, or nothing, just nothing."

Her voice thundered full speed through her description, and when she paused for breath and looked for a reaction, her cheeks were pale and her eyes filled with desperation.

"Do you have any photos of this person?"

"What? No."

Sophie was visibly shaken by the suggestion. She reached out for the arm of her chair, placing one hand down heavily, as if suddenly feeling the need to grip hold of something concrete.

"Is there any chance there's CCTV evidence of someone following you?"

"I went through all this with the police," she said. "Nobody has seen anyone watching me. There aren't any photos or videos. There's no proof at all. Okay? Is that what you want to hear? There's absolutely no evidence to suggest this is anything other than whatever is happening, is only happening in my imagination. There. Satisfied?"

"Sophie, I –"

I was not at all satisfied. I didn't want to see her angry, upset, defensive face. I didn't want any of that.

"Can you think of any reason at all why anyone would want to watch you?"

"Do I not seem like an interesting person?"

Oh Sophie, you're a very interesting person. You're one of the most interesting people I have ever met.

I kept my thoughts to myself.

"That's not what I am saying. Do you think there are any reasons why someone would want to *observe* you?"

"No," she snapped. "No. I'm an ordinary woman with a very ordinary life. I buy most of my clothes in Primark or from supermarkets. I don't have any social media accounts. My main hobbies are reading and watching crappy reality television. Even when Jack was around, we went out two, maybe three times a year. One birthday each and our anniversary. Nowhere fancy, usually wherever we could use a voucher that particular night."

She was clearly doing herself a disservice.

"If there aren't any reasons why someone would want to watch you, it seems unlikely they actually are. Your mind can manifest ideas like this from negative feelings like stress or anxiety and turn those states into paranoia."

"So, if I was clear-headed, and I thought someone was watching me, you would believe me?"

"It's not about what I believe. I work with what you tell me. I'm trying to explain that sometimes the mind can play tricks on us, especially when it's already under pressure." A quick pause. "This all started around the time you lost Jack?"

Sophie nodded.

"Do you see then that there may be a link between what has happened and how you're feeling? Did you ever feel these things before? When Jack was still around?"

She sat quietly, lost in thought, before replying.

"I never *noticed* anything like this. Do you think I should have? Do you think there could have been someone watching me all along?"

"That's not really the point I was trying to make, no."

"When Jack was with me, my life consisted of work and him. I was on autopilot, I suppose."

She stopped in her tracks, making direct eye contact, looking for a response.

"How does that make you feel? "

"It's not the way it sounds. Really it isn't. That almost makes it sound as though I was obsessed with him."

A short laugh slipped from her mouth, and she raised her hand, as though to disguise it.

Obsession. It's an easy trap to fall into.

"He was my husband. He is my husband. I'm supposed to want to be with him, aren't I?"

Her question to herself hung in the air long enough that she began to consider the answer.

"Well. You get the point anyway. I didn't really pay much attention to what was going on around me, I suppose."

"Let me ask you. Are you worried that someone is watching you, or are you worried that you *think* there is someone watching you?"

No reflecting on what she said, no judgement, no exploration. Straight to the point with the most important question. What was it that was troubling her?

Her reaction surprised me. She snorted another sharp laugh and widened her eyes so I could almost see the white above her deep brown irises.

"I hadn't thought about it like that," she said, her face returning to its former serious countenance. "The police, you know, I went to them first. They weren't much help." She shook her head. "That's not true. I'm sure they did everything they could, but..." She held her hands up in a weary shrug. "They said that people choose to disappear all the time. They didn't seem to think there was anything *untoward*." She pronounced the last word as though it tasted sour, and I assumed it was the same word the police used when dismissing her concerns. "I suppose the fact I am here means that I'm more afraid it's all in my head."

"Well, that's something we can explore."

I found myself smiling slightly, but her earnest expression forced me to hold back. I had an uncontrollable urge to reach out and touch her. As she sat, tense and obviously uncomfortable on the brown leather chair, her black, polka-dot speckled skirt rested just above her knees. I wanted to rest my hand there, comforting, reassuring, but of course I couldn't. Instead, I forced myself to lean backwards, physically distancing myself from her further still.

She didn't see anything. She couldn't respond to my thoughts, and I was thankful for that.

She paused again, before saying, her voice softer and more uncertain than previously, "What if I'm losing my mind?"

Oh Sophie. Poor lost, vulnerable Sophie. I want to help you. Helping people is what I do. It's what makes me tick. I don't think there's anything wrong with seeing a troubled woman and wanting to do whatever I can for her. Nurses, doctors, psychiatrists – of course, psychiatrists – all want to make a difference to other people's lives. A positive difference. Looking out for others is a rational, normal thing to do. Doesn't it make sense that someone as needy as Sophie would trigger an intense emotional response in me? Emotional. The more I think about her, the stronger the impulse. For now, I have to keep my feelings in check, stay quiet, and be ready to hear what she has to say. It's almost time. She's almost here. Perhaps today she'll talk about Jack.

CHAPTER THREE

Dear Jack,

Arkhangelsk sounds like a magical place. That name. *Archangel*. It reminds me of that Christmas carol, you know, the one about the hard earth and the bleak winter. That's exactly how I pictured it, like a Christmas card scene with snow-laden trees and endless miles of ice flats.

I flicked through the Wikipedia page and started to learn an entirely new vocabulary. The *tundra*, the *taiga*, the *zapovedniks*: the vast wilderness, and all the ways of describing it. So many different words for bleak emptiness. If Eskimos have fifty words for snow, the Russians have endless ways of describing barren wastelands.

It just wasn't *you*. We weren't Arctic people, you and me. You would wear your winter coat in August if it didn't look so ridiculous. I don't know how you thought you were going to cope in the Arctic Circle.

I know it was a prestigious posting for you, that you had to fight off the competition to get it, but somehow, I thought getting the opportunity would be enough. I thought you wanted to be *offered* the post, not actually take it. I never made the connection, as stupid as it might sound. I thought you were excited about your success, and I was happy for you. Genuinely, I was. But as for actually going...

From the moment you told me, it was as though you'd opened a floodgate. Arkhangelsk was all you could talk about.

Remember when you pulled out that map like you were in some fantasy novel going on a mythical adventure to find the one ring or however it goes. Again, that's something you know more about than I ever did, but that's not the point. You elevated your posting to fantastical proportions. It was a life-changing opportunity, an important geological mission. To me, it was, just as all your other trips had been, a few weeks away looking at rocks.

"If you tried harder to understand, you'd get it," you would tell me. As if it were a lack of understanding that was stopping me from being interested.

I never cared about rocks. I cared about being with you, and your work stopped me from doing that. Rocks were my nemeses. How sad is that?

You spread the map, crisp, new, and fresh from its protective plastic packaging, onto our old, worn kitchen table, covering up the traces of our solid, well-used life with your plans for the future. I watched, detached, but trying to show some enthusiasm, as you tried to locate the Arkhangelsk Oblast. You overshot, jabbing your finger somewhere along the northern coast of Russia, perhaps a thousand miles from your actual intended location.

After some probing, you found the spider-web of Moscow and took your bearings from there. North, north, north to the edge of the White Sea. The name *Arkhangelsk* further towards the Pole, that fantasy-like snow-buried landscape. The bleak midwinter. Magical hot chocolate and conjured Turkish delight. Animals turned to stone by an evil witch, and you there, picking at those stones, trying to uncover the meaning inside.

You did your best to involve me as you gathered your kit together, shopped for warm clothes, thick socks, and the kind of specialist boots they don't sell in Foot Locker. The more equipment and clothing that started to fill the shed, the more concrete and inescapable the truth became. You were going to Russia, and there was nothing I could do about it.

Or at least that's what I thought then.

I can't write any more.

Soph

CHAPTER FOUR

Even though Henny or Lola have obviously told her she can enter the room, Sophie gives a sharp three-rap knock on the door and waits for permission. I can just see her, standing there in that dark rose-coloured jacket of hers, hair scooped up into a pony tail she probably doesn't intend to be nearly as messy as it always looks. There's something about her that screams of trying hard but just missing the mark, and it's adorable. I wait, of course, savouring the few moments of anticipation before she walks into the office.

She's already slipping her arms out of the sleeves of her jacket as she comes in. It's mid-July, too hot for the clothes she's chosen, but I can tell she's aiming for smart and stylish rather than dressing for the season. It's a minor point, but, as they say, it's the little things that matter. Picking

up on these details can tell you a lot about someone. Paying attention to the minutiae can help you
understand a person, and I want to understand Sophie.

She stands, jacket draped over one arm, waiting again for permission to sit or an invitation to
speak.

"Hang it over the back of the chair and take a
seat."

She does what she's told, and sits with her pale,
bare legs crossed at the ankles.

Those little black ballet pumps she's wearing
have obviously been chosen to match the prim A-
line skirt that's resting above her knees. I'm almost taken in by her formal, considered appearance, but I know it's all for show. She's doing her
best to look like a woman who has got herself together, even though she's in a psychiatrist's office. If she met one of her colleagues in the street
on the way to her appointment, I'm almost certain

she could convince them she was popping out for a visit to her masseur rather than to see her shrink.

I'm looking in the wrong place though, and that's a rookie mistake. She wears oval-framed glasses, with a tortoiseshell finish that works well with the red-brown colour of her hair. Today, they also highlight the redness of her eyes. She's been crying, and recently. They aren't the bloodshot remnants of a sobbing session at home. They're evidence of tears shed in the minutes, perhaps moments, before her arrival. Her skin looks pasty and dry, and although she's done her best to cover her sallow complexion with make-up, I can see the powder on her cheeks and the traces of mascara that have settled beneath her eyes. In different circumstances, I may have leaned towards her, offered her a cigarette, or a strong drink, but of course I can't do that. Instead, I look at her, taking in her appearance, and think about exactly how I can help her.

This is session number three, and it's about time she opened up, if she really wants things to change.

This week's starter question is a catch-all: *"What's been happening?"*

Sophie inhales a long, shaky breath, her red eyes turned down, doing her best to avoid eye contact.

I think, for a moment, that she's about to start crying again. She's wavering, hesitant and unsteady. Seeing her like this, it's difficult to believe Sophie is a professional woman herself. Even though she's taken the first part of this year as a long-term leave of absence, she's a fully qualified and moderately experienced professional. As she wrote the word "teacher" in her looping oversized handwriting on the form Henny gave her to complete rather than checking the box for "unemployed", one can only assume she plans, someday, to return to that profession.

She speaks, but I'm so lost in my thoughts, I miss what she says.

I need to focus. Stop thinking about the Sophie of the past – Sophie of the future maybe – and concentrate on the here and now. Isn't that the advice I would give to her too?

"I haven't been out much," she says. "I don't want to leave the house. Every time I go out, I'm looking over my shoulder. People must think I'm crazy. *I* think I'm crazy."

"And you feel safe at home?"

"Our house... my house is a fortress. It's so secure that if I ever got locked out, I'd probably have to move. Jack was good on that front, at least. He said if he had to go away and leave me alone for weeks at a time, he wanted to be sure I was safe. You can walk up the path to the front door, but after that, there's no hope of getting in. Unless I let you." She smiles at that little add on sentence, pleased with her joke, but the smile doesn't stay for long. She pulls her lips back into a tight frown, as though displeased with herself for being anything other than negative. "Jack wanted to keep me safe. He loved me, you know."

I can't take my eyes off her. I don't want to miss anything else that she says. It feels like we are finally getting to the root of her issues.

"You know, I wish I could understand what they want from me. Why they're watching me, following me, whatever. I don't get it. It doesn't make any sense."

"Has anything happened since you were here last week? You seem very certain right now that there is someone following you. Last week when we talked, you were considering the idea this might be something you're imagining. How does that idea feel to you now?"

"Yes. I know. I know I was *considering* that," she says, stressing the word. "But I'm also very much considering someone is following me, watching everything I do, and tracking every move I make."

Slow, steady nod. Take in the words. Try not to show an immediate response. Good.

"It's quite common for people who have been subjected to a traumatic experience or a period of stress or anxiety to develop persecutory delusions."

"What, sorry?"

"Persecutory delusions. Delusional disorder is a kind of mental disturbance that can happen to people such as yourself who have suffered a significant negative life event."

"Is that what they call it now? Losing your husband? *A 'significant negative life event'?*" Sophie makes a short, ironic laugh.

"You have some of the other signs one might expect to see in someone with this type of psychosis."

"Psychosis, is it?" She shakes her head slowly but manages to keep eye contact. "I lost my husband. I'm not about to go out on a mass killing spree or…"

"It's not a derogatory term, Sophie. These labels are designed to help us put together the signs and symptoms, unpick your feelings and concerns and try to find the best way forward to help to make you better."

"How long will it take me to get better?" she asks.

The answer is necessarily vague.

"Better? It depends on what you mean by better. Better than you are now? You could feel better when you leave here today."

"*Better* better," she says, and I know what she means. Still, there is no simple answer.

"What does better mean to you? What do you want to achieve?"

Questions as answers – the staple of a psychiatrist's toolkit.

I sit in silence, waiting for her response. She sits in silence, not giving one.

Instead, she looks around the room, taking in the setting, probably trying to work out how she, a previously well-balanced thirtysomething year old, has ended up in psychiatric therapy. It's a reasonable thought to have. Who expects their mental health will take such a nosedive that they need professional help? Sure, we all have bad days, and I've probably had more than most, but being referred for psychiatric therapy, well…

There's not all that much for her to look at in the room. On the surface, it's set up to appear comfortable and non-clinical. Of course, there's a solid desk, kept clear between patient visits in the spirit of tidy desk, tidy mind. I'm sure there's some message there from the Marie Kondo school of mental health care, but the truth is probably closer to protecting the need for confidentiality. The last thing a psychiatrist wants is for one patient to be reading the case notes of another. Everyone has their own special little bundle of issues.

Woe betide they cross the streams and get caught up in each other's drama.

The seating arrangement in the office is designed to create balance. Patient and professional have the same chairs. I'm no better and no worse than you. Let's be equals. In practice, that means we both have faux leather armchair seats. Comfy, but not too cosy. You wouldn't want to sit in that chair for too long, but it's supposed to make you feel relaxed enough to open your mind and open your mouth. Subtly, of course. Subconsciously.

The only other clues to the purpose of the room are the two wall-to-ceiling bookcases against the back wall. They're positioned behind the patient's seat, so there's no chance of them getting distracted trying to read the small print on the spines while they are trying to avoid talking. Behind the psychiatrist's chair is the window, but the blinds are always drawn just enough to let the light through whilst preventing anyone from looking in or out.

Unlike your standard NHS general practice clinical setting, there are no posters on the wall. No reminders to wash your hands, check your breasts or make sure you phone to cancel an appointment if you can't make it. Once you're in the room, it's all about the session. Besides, if you forget to cancel your appointment, you're paying for it anyway, so why would anyone want to remind you?

Finally, Sophie snaps me from my own thoughts with her reply.

"I want to feel like I'm not…" she pauses, trying to choose the right word. "Crazy. Nuts. I don't know. I hate those words, but I hate feeling like this. Wow, how did I even…" Her voice trails off, and she shakes her head with a slow, disbelieving sadness.

I can't hazard a guess at how long it might take for her. She's a complicated woman, a complicated case.

"Tell me about how you're feeling now."

"I feel like I'm losing my mind. They told me, the police told me there was no evidence that anyone was watching me – is watching me – following me, stalking me, whatever. At first, they sounded sympathetic, but the more I called, they lost that edge, and I think I was on the verge of getting arrested for wasting police time. That's crazy. That's what crazy is."

"So, you went to talk to your doctor?"

"I was already talking to him. I have trouble sleeping when Jack's away sometimes, and after, well, I was struggling."

Rifle through the case file, nod and try not to distract her from her stream of consciousness.

"I didn't feel like it was a medical thing, you know. Medical. Psychological. Whatever. I didn't want drugs, I just wanted sleep."

I make a mental note. No medications,

"You seem like an intelligent woman, Sophie."

She raises her eyebrows and lets out a short *hmmpfh* sound of disagreement.

"No, really. You're educated; you're a teacher, aren't you?"

"I was. Before all this."

"Assuming all this is temporary, you *are* a teacher, aren't you?"

Sophie shrugs. "I guess so, yeah."

"Okay then. So, tell me this: what reason would there be for anyone to want to follow you?"

It's clearly not something she has an immediate response for. She tightens her lips, dips her eyes down in thought, and remains silent, thinking of an appropriate reply.

"People do that, don't they? Stalkers? Serial killers? I don't know. You see it on the news, read about it, whatever."

"Read about it in books? Like fiction?"

"No. I mean, not just fiction. It happens, doesn't it? Women walking home, going about their usual business, and then…"

She makes a vague gesture with her hands, but I understand the meaning.

"They disappear? Something bad happens to them?"

"Yes, that. I don't want to say it. I don't want to think about it, because I don't want it to happen to me."

"And that's what you're afraid of? Someone is following you because they want to hurt you?"

Just a nod.

"And this has been happening for how long?"

"Ever since, well, it started not long after... after I lost... Seven months. It's been seven months."

"And in all that time, has anyone physically threatened you? Has anyone contacted you? Approached you?"

She lets out a long, deep sigh and concedes, "No. Nothing like that."

39

Rather than the relief of feeling that perhaps she is not in danger after all, she has an appearance of defeat.

"Hey. Sophie. This is good news. It might be scary for you to think what you're experiencing is psychological, but psychological is something we can deal with."

Slowly, she nods her head and says, so quietly I have to strain to hear her, "I hope so. I really hope so."

There's a silence before she speaks again.

"I have a theory," she says. I can't stop myself from jumping to attention to hear what she has to say. "I think, maybe, one of the reasons I feel this way is guilt." She shakes her head as soon as she's spoken the word. "Not guilt for anything I've done. I mean…" Sophie sighs and carries on as though she doesn't want to. "When the police came. Well, it's not that they held me personally responsible or anything, but they were just like, so dismissive.

He's a big boy now and maybe he just decided he didn't want to be with you anymore, Mrs Portman.

Of course, no one actually said that, but they didn't have to."

"And what do you think about that?"

"What?"

"What do you think about the idea that Jack might have disappeared of his own free will?"

"I think it sounds..." she stops, trying to find the next word, and as usual I sit patiently and let her come to it. Eventually, she speaks the most calm, clear word she has said all session: "Impossible."

CHAPTER FIVE

Dearest Jack,

Three sessions into therapy and I'm going round in circles. I know you would be proud of me for going though, so I'm going to stick it out. At least for now.

Doctor Thacker is very patiently putting up with my silences and stupidity. I mustn't talk about myself like that, I know. That's what you would tell me. I feel like a child though, sitting there in front of him, while he expects me to bare my soul.

I'm not sure you would like him much. He's one of those *my-other-car-is-a-Range-Rover* types you see in bars with their craft beers and identically dressed friends. The kind you would nod your head over at and give me that wry *there's-another-one* smile. We always enjoyed people-watching, which seems ironic now, given the circumstances.

I feel like I've been alone for such a long time. Not just since you've not been around, but before that. You were only home from New York for three weeks before the Arkhangelsk trip came up. I'm sure you knew about it for months. I can imagine you carrying the idea around with you, not wanting to tell me, like a pregnant woman, not wanting to share the news until she's out of the woods and in the safe zone. Safe zones are never really completely safe, though, are they? Nothing is.

To you, these field trips were opportunities, all part of your rise to glory. To me, they were weeks alone without you. Italy, Spain, Mexico, the names of countries began to lose meaning. All they symbolised was that you weren't at home again.

Oh, but you should have known this would happen. You knew when you met me that my dreams would take me around the world.

I knew when I met you that you had dreams of travelling the world, making it to the top of your career, being the best. I didn't know you would put those dreams ahead of your relationship with me. I didn't know when we got together and planned our own joint future that it was meant to fit around the plans you already had. Even when you were here, you spent so much time out in your shed preparing for the next great mission that I was still alone. Your vision was that of a young, single adventurer, and I was more of a stay-at-home than a tag-along. I don't think I was ever meant to be your sidekick.

You had your dreams too.

That's what you would tell me. I was training to be a teacher when we met. It was all I had ever wanted to do, to step into my mother's footsteps and follow her into the job I had seen her love all of her short life. It wasn't so much of a dream as it was my destiny.

I know you would shrug your shoulders and shake your head at me and tell me it all came down to the same thing. I chose my path, and you chose yours.

We were walking in parallel lines, side by side, forwards in life. The only problem with parallel lines is that they never touch.

Enough for now.

Soph

CHAPTER SIX

"Good morning, Henny," I call in as cheerful a tone as I can drag up.

She flicks her eyes up in my direction and turns straight back down to the desk. Her only response is a forced grunt. I've done something to annoy her, or someone else has done something to annoy her, and I'm on the receiving end of it.

Lola pokes her colleague gently. Not that gently, because Henny makes a second grunt, higher pitched this time.

"Good morning, sir," Lola smiles.

She's looking good today, in her low-cut strappy top. Professional, but cute all the same. I wonder if she lives alone and make a note to ask her next time Henny's not around. Not that I'm interested in her in any kind of romantic or sexual way. Even if I were, I don't think it would be appropriate, what with her being the assistant and all. These thoughts run through my mind, and I don't let any of them show in my facial expression. It's a trick I've learned, that poker-face facade.

"Good morning," I repeat, mirroring her words.

I'd love to stop and chat to her, but I'm running late already, so I head straight into the office.

It's too hot, too stuffy. Nine in the morning, just after, and the sun has already managed to heat up the fake leather chairs to the point of scorching discomfort. There's no air, but the windows don't open, and this building is too old for air con. Put up and shut up.

Thursday morning and it's Jonah Washington's turn in the hot seat. Thirty-three years old and a complete basket case. Of course, that's not the politically correct term, and it's definitely not the recognised diagnostic description. Borderline personality disorder is the technical phrase, but borderline makes it sound as though it's a so-so condition, perching on the edge of normal and ab-normal. I'm not keen on it, but who cares what I think? That's the diagnosis, and the treatment is this tedious programme of therapy. This and the medication anyway.

The sessions always start the same way: an invitation to talk. I lean back in my chair without making it too obvious I'm settling in for the duration. I've not had a chance to touch the tea either Henny or Lola left for me – Lola, judging by Hen's attitude this morning – and I don't want to reach out for it now. I don't want to distract him or take his attention away from the conversation. I can wait. I will have to wait.

It's probably not very professional, but I want to ask, "Did you notice anything off about Henny today?" The question is like an itch beneath my skin as we discuss the usual trivialities that are designed to gather information, paint a picture of the patient's progress, or lack of it.

"Tell me about your week."

As vague, generic openings go, it's one of my least favourites. The answer can be anything from a ramble about the queuing time in Lidl to a detailed report of hours of sobbing and suicidal thoughts. It's never like this with Sophie. There's always a relaxed, easy segue from her arrival to the start of the session, like it's a normal, natural chat between friends rather than a session with a psychiatrist.

He sits in silence, looking at me, as though I'm going to do all the work. Always the same.

"Not very exciting," is the eventual response.

"Okay. Can you tell me about what's been happening?"

"Nothing much."

I manage to stifle a frustrated sigh.

"Have you been keeping the diet journal we talked about?"

Binge eating is somewhere near the bottom of the list of concerns, but it's something to focus on. It's not so much that it's an easy win, but when you have as many issues as Jonah Washington, you have to start somewhere.

"Sure. I've been eating the same trash. I sit in my chair, order takeout, get up to collect it from the door, sit back down and stuff my face. Isn't that what everyone does now? Isn't that just modern society?"

Is it?

"Well, to some extent, yes. When it becomes part of someone's obsessive nature, though, it's definitely worth keeping track of. We discussed this last week, didn't we?"

We did, but good old Jonah wants to go over everything again every week. That's his whole *thing*, isn't it? He's more than happy to run his mouth once he gets going, but he never achieves anything from one week to the next. He knows what his problems are, but he's not putting in the work to address them.

"We did."

At least he can acknowledge it.

"Jonah, you know I want to help you."

"Uh-huh."

"And I can only do that if you are prepared to help yourself."

"Sure."

The clock shows twenty past the hour and we are set to talk until ten to. Clients never get a full hour for their money; there's always wrapping up and winding down, and booking them in for the next session. It's standard practice, no one is trying to pull a fast one, but right now it means the two of us have half an hour to fill with productive conversation. Two thirty-something year old men, one a six-foot-tall blonde with stubble that could pass for designer, and the other a few inches shorter, dark hair, dark eyes, and clothes that most certainly have never seen an ironing board. Guess who's who?

The blonde man observes the dark man, and the dark man sits silently. Thursdays are hard work and both of us know it.

51

"I'll do it this week. I promise."

"Okay. You know this is to help you, don't you? I'm not here to judge you. That's not what you're paying me for."

A swift smile, an attempt to lighten the mood, but it goes unreturned.

"As long as I keep paying you, you'll keep seeing me, won't you? Even if we aren't getting anywhere."

That's definitely worth a smile.

"We are getting somewhere, Jonah. We will get somewhere."

"Somewhere, sure. I really don't think you know where that somewhere is though."

We lock eyes again, almost two stags facing off, ready to lock horns. Almost, apart from the imbalance in our relationship. For all intents, we are two regular men, each with our own issues, each with our own lives and the joys and problems they entail. One of us needs to pay for psychiatric care, and one of us gets paid to give it.

CHAPTER SEVEN

The more time I spend in the office, the less interesting I find myself. When I leave, I try to sound cheerful in my goodbyes to Lola and Henny, but they're too wrapped up in each other and whatever conversation I've interrupted to even give me a wave. I try not to take it personally, but I can't help but think if I were them, I wouldn't want to talk to me either.

I used to be an interesting man, with a steady, attractive girlfriend, and a job I adored. Now I'm living for my hourly slots with a woman I admittedly barely know. Explaining how it came to this, how I slipped from stability to my own kind of borderline obsession, well, it's complicated. That saying, *'you always want what you haven't got,'* sums up how this all began, though.

I shouldn't complain about the job. I'm doing exactly what I wanted to do ever since I remember. I set my sights on what I wanted and worked my butt off to get to where I am today. Of course, I wanted more. I want more. There aren't many opportunities for furthering my career now. I'm doing the best I can, and that sounds exactly the way I intended it. I live a single-serving life, and that one serving is stale.

As for the girlfriend, well, Serena was perfect in many ways, but the longer I was with her, the less I wanted to be with her. On the surface, she was a perfect match for me: ambitious, caring, and patient. But when I dug a little deeper, I found the strata of rot running through her.

Everything ended, as everything tends to do. For once, it wasn't my fault. At least not directly. Who knows how much of an impact my peachy personality had on her decision to start seeing someone else? If I could have changed myself, maybe it wouldn't have happened. If I were enough, perhaps she and I would still be together. My life could be filled with dinner parties, dates at restaurants and the kind of sex you don't have to pay for. I've been alone for a year; I've learned how to fit into my existence. Just about.

When I met Sophie, I got a glimpse into another world, a realm of possibilities, a whole different life. If I had to put my finger on it, I'd say it's her effortlessness that draws me to her. She is what she is. She's not afraid to be herself, do what needs to be done. It might not look like it, seeing her sitting in the psychiatrist's chair, but Sophie is a strong woman. The trick is going to be getting her to see that, getting her to believe it. If I can help her to do that, well, who knows? The woman clearly has issues. Of course she does. No one would pay to talk to a psychiatrist if they didn't have to. I'm not saying that she's perfect, but she's perfect to me. That's what matters.

Let me get one thing clear though: however infatuated by her I am - and I admit that's what it is, infatuation - I'm not stalking Sophie. I see her during her sessions, once a week, and that's as far as it goes. If there *is* someone following her, it's not me.

I'm sure I would be seen as the prime suspect, the way I go on about her – at least I would be if I actually talked about my feelings to anyone else. Who would I tell, though?

It's not like I talk to anybody about anything outside of that office. What I say during sessions is of no interest to anyone outside those four walls, and my chats with Henny and Lola are hardly noteworthy. I listen closely, and I watch carefully, but only when Sophie is at the office.

I live on my own in this dull, over-priced apartment. I don't have any friends to speak of, and my weekly phone calls to my mother dwindled to the biannual birthday and Christmas greetings so long ago that I don't even remember how we let them slide. That is, effectively, the story of my life. Things happen to me. I'm an object, not a subject.

From what I know, Sophie's single-serving life is not terribly different from my own. I haven't experienced loss in the same way as her, but all the same, I did lose someone too. Is there any difference between losing someone to the Arctic and losing someone to another person? In some ways, yes, and in others, no. Loss is loss. Either way, it's a bereavement of sorts. We all have to deal with it in our own ways.

I saw the signs in my disintegrating relationship months before the end. I was tied up in my work, married to my job – and never married to Serena. That's not to say I wouldn't have popped the question eventually, if things hadn't happened the way they did, but we grew further apart rather than closer together. It was like the sea receding before the coming of a tsunami. There was nothing between us for a time, and then, suddenly, we were destroyed. I should have seen the signs, and perhaps I could have done something to save us. I know from watching too much television that if you see the sea disappear, you should run for high ground. I have all kinds of useless information stored in my head about how to deal with disasters and dangers and other unlikely events, but I had no idea how to save our relationship. By the time I knew what was happening, it was too late. I was already drowning.

Serena had started going to the gym, which is fine, of course. Can't argue with someone wanting to better themselves, or just feel good about who they are. I thought *I* was making her feel good, but that didn't quite turn out to be the truth.

If I remember correctly, and I admit I might not, the beginning of the end went a little like this:

Picture the two of us in our perfectly feng-shiued flat. I was in the hallway, heading to the bedroom. Neither of us had been home from work long, but despite being tired, I was ready for the night ahead. Serena, on the other hand, seemed to have forgotten our plans.

She was in the bathroom, washing her face with some of that face scrub that cost too much for me to use any of it. I found that out the hard way when I borrowed a squirt one day. I seemed to make mistakes constantly without even knowing it.

"Date night," I reminded her with my most endearing look.

Without turning from the mirror, Serena sighed and said, "Can we reschedule?" I saw the pained look on her face in her reflection.

Her hair was already tied into a tight, drawn back ponytail, the kind she would never wear unless she was planning on working out. She was a natural kind of woman, she barely wore makeup, and let her hair float around her shoulders. Serena dressed for comfort rather than fashion and it suited her. There was no need for her to make any more effort because she was already perfect to me.

"Okay." I tried to hide my disappointment; I didn't want her to feel bad when she was doing something positive for herself. What kind of a monster would that have made me? I wanted to be a loving, supportive partner. That's my real dream job – more important than my career, more important than my own feelings – but I couldn't be a supportive partner without a partner to support.

"Come on," she said. I mustn't have done a good enough acting job. "Don't be like that."

And that's how arguments start. Misinterpretation, miscommunication. The simplest look can lead to disaster. All those little earthquakes can trigger the kind of seismic shift that sets off that final tsunami. Big endings have to start somewhere.

That doesn't matter now. Serena is as lost as Jack is. Now, I am alone in the house we once shared. Nothing but the chair and the screen to keep me company.

Seeing Sophie is a step towards filling the void in my life. She's not a stand-in or a replacement for Serena, she's a more perfect version of her. She's the Serena that will never leave me.

I won't make any mistakes this time. Not with Sophie. This time, everything is going to be perfect.

CHAPTER EIGHT

I managed to send myself into a whirlpool of dark-
ness, thinking about what I had, and what I want
but don't have yet. By the time Tuesday morning
finally arrives, I'm practically on the edge of my
seat waiting for Sophie to show.

It might sound silly, but I got up especially
early so I could have a shower, style my hair and
step into fresh, ironed clothes today. There's no
way she will see what I've done for her, but it
makes me feel good knowing I've made an effort.
I can't change what she thinks or feels, but I can
make the best of myself. I'd *like* to change what
she thinks and feels, of course. That's essentially
why she's attending therapy sessions, after all.

While I'm waiting for her to arrive, I make myself comfortable in my chair, trying to find the
best way to position myself to observe her. The
patient's chair is at an angle to the psychiatrist's,

rather than the two of them being head-on. It's designed to feel less confrontational for the patient, but I'm not sure how effective that is. The room is obviously a clinical setting, even though it's been set up to look relaxing and welcoming. The carpet is a thick, plush brown to match the faux leather of the chairs, the walls are papered in a light cream pattern-free style, the kind you might see in a show home rather than in a clinical environment. It's a room with purpose, and one of the purposes is to try to trick the patient into forgetting what its primary purpose is: psychiatric therapy.

My mind has wandered to this deconstruction of interior design, mainly because Sophie is late. The clock says it's two minutes past nine, and it has no reason to lie. If only the patients were as honest and reliable as the clock. If only they made as much progress. Time is always moving forward. Patients can also shift backwards, sideways and sometimes get nowhere.

Neither Henny nor Lola have been in to say Sophie has cancelled, and I can't hear enough of what's going on in the reception area to know whether she's arrived and is lagging out there for some reason. My own personal brand of anxiety is starting to kick in, the light panic that perhaps I won't see her today, when the three taps on the door ring out.

I know it's Sophie. I should never have doubted her, not for a second. I would apologise for my thoughts if it wasn't such a ridiculous idea.

When she finally walks into the room, I can't hide my smile.

Her jacket is draped over her arm, like a comfort blanket. It's too warm now to wear it, but it seems somehow she can't bring herself to leave it at home.

"I'm so sorry," she says. "I overslept my alarm."

"No problem. It's fine. Take a seat."

The words are redundant, as she's already moving to sit down. Even though she's late, there's still time for a quick exchange of pleasantries before moving on to the heavy stuff. Ease her into it gently and all that.

"How have things been this week?"

Sophie leans back in her chair, looking more comfortable than I've ever seen her until now. It's strangely disconcerting.

"I don't want to jinx anything, but you know, I think I have been a little better."

I didn't expect to hear this so soon, especially when she was still convinced last week that she was being followed. I'm not sure I fully believe her, yet her body language is relaxed, and she's even bringing out her deadly smile.

"Well, that's good to hear. Tell me more."

"More?"

"About how you're feeling. What is it that's changed?"

She looks as though she was unprepared for this line of questioning. Perhaps she thought that she would come in, sit down, say that everything is fine now, and that would be it. Wouldn't it be lovely if that were the case? I'd love for Sophie to come to terms with what happened, to move forward and build a happy life again. But I don't see it happening quite this quickly.

"I haven't seen anyone this week," she says. "Following me, I mean. Watching me. I haven't been out of the house much, but when I have been, I've not noticed anyone. I haven't even had those feelings, you know, that someone is there. I don't know. Maybe I'm just accepting there wasn't anyone in the first place. That, you know, the problem is…" She taps a finger against her temple, but her meaning was already clear. "Or maybe whoever is watching me is on holiday this week. Could be either." She smiles at her own attempt at dark humour, and I can't stop myself from following suit.

Good. Good. Still, I want to hear more.

"Uh huh." It's a prompt to continue more than a response.

She settles back to seriousness and carries on talking. "I don't know. I was thinking, after our last session, that I wasn't getting anywhere. It was like I was going round in circles. You know, the thoughts in my head, and when I'm here talking to you. I go round and round and get nowhere. As long as I keep fixating on the idea someone is watching me, I don't think I can start to get better. The more I think about everything, the more I wonder: what if I *have* been wrong all this time, and I *am* imagining it? I think I might have to let go of the idea that I'm being watched before I can deal with the real issue."

"What do you think the real issue is?"

One of the tricks a psychiatrist can use is to pick out key words and throw them back at the patient. They might have a vague idea of what *'real issue'* means, but it's unlikely they can verbalise the meaning. Asking the question, reflecting the phrase, can force the patient to think more deeply about what they've said. It's a challenge, getting them to explain their own thoughts.

"Right," she says, nodding, as though she's agreeing, rather than that she has been asked a difficult question. "It's obvious, really. This all began with what happened with Jack. That's when I started to feel this way. So, since he's not been around, I think that's really when I started to become…" She searches for a word, and then throws one out as a suggestion, or maybe a question. "Anxious?"

Nod. Silence. Wait for more.

"Paranoid," she stumbles, tentatively.

"Okay."

Not getting much of a response, she searches for more words, more possible definitions for her issues.

"Delusional?" she asks, less certainly.

The words flutter in the air, and they need time to fall and sink in. After a long, silent minute, it's time to start unpicking her conclusions.

"Is that what you think you're facing here, then? Anxiety? Paranoia? Delusions?"

She laughs nervously. "You're the psychiatrist," she says. "You tell me. They're all words you used before, last time. Isn't that what's going on here? You know, *'significant life event'*, *'traumatic experience'*?"

She tries to affect a deep, masculine inflection as she repeats the phrases. Her memory is more accurate than her accent. Those were the words from the last session.

"How does that feel to you? Thinking about your situation in those terms?"

"Well, I want something to work with. You know? I haven't seen anyone watching me, even though I've been looking out, trying to catch them. The police must be right after all. Makes sense really. So, if there isn't anybody watching

69

me, I *must* be imagining it. At least once I accept that I'm crazy, I can get some help, right?"

I'm nodding, but the selfish side of me is already thinking I don't want her to get better, I want her to keep coming to these sessions so I can keep seeing her. I've got to push those thoughts out of my head. There's no way I can let myself think along those lines. She won't be leaving for a while yet. Just because she thinks she knows what her problems are, it doesn't mean she'll be fixed immediately. Fixed. Like a broken arm in a plaster cast, a blood transfusion for low haemoglobin. Why can't there be a quick solution for mental health issues?

Perhaps medication would be a step in the right direction.

"The report from your GP says that you haven't tried any pharmacological treatment yet."

The drugs usually come before the therapy sessions, not the other way round. I can see Sophie's reluctance reflected in her sinking shoulders.

"Was there a particular reason you didn't go down that route?"

"It seems like such a big step. I mean, okay, coming for psychiatric therapy is massive, sure, but I don't know. Taking drugs feels so..." She searches for the word, but doesn't find it, and offers a shake of her head instead.

"I appreciate there can be a misconception that being prescribed mental health medication is stigmatising, but I think you'll find that society is much more accepting these days."

Probably because such a significant percentage of society are actually taking mental health medications of some kind or another. It's okay not to be okay.

She forces a small, tight smile, but doesn't reply.

"If you had a migraine, what would you do?"

"I can see where you're going with this," she says. "But it's not the same, is it? Anyone can go into Tesco and pick up a packet of ibuprofen and self-medicate. You don't need a prescription to get something for your headache."

"Not the minor ones, no. Okay, think of it another way. If you broke a bone, you'd agree to a plaster cast."

"I wouldn't be happy about it, but yeah."

"You *have* experienced a significant life event." That phrase again. "You *are* experiencing symptoms that could be related to stress and anxiety as a result of that life event. If we can treat those underlying problems, perhaps we can make a start on reducing their effects. The significant life event was the equivalent of your fall from a tree. The stress and anxiety-related symptoms are your broken bone. The medication is your plaster cast. It's going to help to guide you in the right direction toward healing. Along with these sessions, of course."

"What I'm seeing, or feeling, or whatever could be a result of anxiety?"

"Or stress. More than that, perhaps. It's possible you're going through post-traumatic stress. Your brain is trying to process your loss, and it's struggling to put things into perspective. If I prescribe you some medication, the pills could help your brain to do its job and set you back on the right track."

"And I wouldn't need to come here anymore?" She half-smiles at her half-joke, and I have to smile too. She can be funny when she's not so uptight. If I could make her smile more often, she wouldn't have to keep turning up for the therapy sessions she clearly doesn't enjoy.

"I think it's best if you try the meds and carry on with these sessions too. Maybe the combination of both is the best way forward. Would you be willing to try that?"

Sophie nods with a slow, solemn sureness.

"Yes," she says. "The truth is, I can't stand feeling this way. It's difficult enough being on my own, not having Jack here with me. Some days I

73

can hardly cope. All of this…" She raises her hand to her head and makes a little circling motion, the universal sign for instability. "It's too much. Just too much."

"Okay." Calm, reassuring. "Let's try it. See how it goes. Okay?"

Again, that nod, this time with a timid smile of acceptance. Something in her vulnerability makes her more beautiful than ever. If I could, I would reach out and stroke her pale cheek, feel the warmth of her flesh against my fingers. I'm afraid I wouldn't be able to stop there, that I would grip her face, pull her towards me and push my lips against hers. I'd be powerless as soon as my skin made contact with hers. I can't do that now. I can't touch her. One day, though. One day, I'm going to do more than just look at her. One day, and that one day is going to come soon.

I let the thoughts settle and turn my eyes away from her. The clock ticks, and from beyond the door comes the muffled sound of Henny and Lola's chatter. I can't make out what they are talking about, and I don't want to be distracted from Sophie by attempting to eavesdrop. All I want is to let the silence hang while I watch her and wait for her words.

After the minute hand has advanced once and then again, she remains silent. I'm not sure whether it's time for the question that follows, but she's not started to talk about it on her own yet. It's been a positive session; Sophie has made progress. Perhaps she's ready.

A quiet clearing of the throat and then the question we've all been waiting for.

"Do you think it might be helpful to talk about what happened?"

"Happened?"

"With Jack." The words are tentative. I'm less sure now, more apprehensive. This could easily backfire. "So far, we've been talking about your feelings, but it seems to me that what you're experiencing now all stems from what happened at the end of last year. With Jack."

The change in Sophie's demeanour is instantaneous. It would be a cliché to say that the colour drains from her face, but that is almost, quite literally, the truth. She says nothing but doesn't break eye contact. Instead, her hand reaches out to her side and fumbles against the desk. It looks like she's trying to grasp onto something for support; she's floundering.

"I know it's going to be hard for you, but I don't think we can progress without exploring what happened."

"'Happened' is such a simple word, isn't it?" she says. Her voice is feather light. She's a fragile bird, in danger of being blown away.

It's difficult, sometimes, trying to avoid trigger words, trying not to say things that upset or anger people. What you might think is actually a remarkably simple, straightforward word can have a negative effect on another person.

"Okay, okay…"

It's too late. Sophie is rising to her feet, stretching her flapping hand to the floor to pick up her bag.

"Sophie. Sit down. It's alright. You're alright."

"I am *not* alright. I am far from alright. I have wasted a whole month coming here, talking around what is *really* important. I thought I was getting somewhere today. I actually felt good, just for a few minutes. And now you want me to talk about Jack," she says, pulling on her jacket, "I can't. I just… I can't."

There's a heavy, sick feeling in my gut and I have to swallow it down. I don't want to see her like this. No matter how much she needs to unburden the truth, perhaps today is not the day. I'm standing up before my brain catches up with my actions, reaching towards her, unsteady, out of control.

"I have to go," she says flatly, concealing her emotion far better than I can. "I'm sorry for wasting your time."

"Sophie." I speak her name, but it falls into an empty room.

CHAPTER NINE

My first instinct is to yell expletives, slam out of my chair and race out to find Sophie, apologise for everything. That would be the easiest thing to do, but none of what is happening to her is my fault. I have nothing to be sorry for. If she can't face up to her own issues, it's not on me. Still, that doesn't mean I want her to leave. Quite the opposite. I'm here for her, to listen, observe and wait. I always have her best interests at heart, whether she knows that or not.

Her name is on the tip of my tongue, like a diver waiting to leap from a high board. I want to spit it, to force it out, shout it, make it shoot from my mouth, but instead I let it tumble quietly through my lips.

Sophie.

The word comes out sounding like a compliment rather than a curse, but the last thing I want is to be sitting alone in this room saying her name.

My temples pound with the pressure of my elevated pulse. This is not good. Not good at all.

I know what I need to do. I've been through the process so many times that it's my go-to when I start feeling anxious now. I force myself to take calming breaths, feel the air enter through my nose, deep and slow, and exit as a long sighing burst through my mouth. In and out, focusing only on the process of breathing as my pounding heart rate gradually settles into a regular pattern.

It takes five minutes, maybe ten, until my body stutters into a calm equilibrium. Even though I'm back in control, all I can think about is her. One person shouldn't be able to have this effect upon another, but Sophie is unique.

I'm expecting her to open up and be honest during her sessions, but it's not as though I'm doing that either. I can't judge her for holding back

80

and keeping secrets when I'm doing the same thing, too.

It's not easy to explain how or why I'm so invested in this woman. Since I first set eyes upon her, I knew she could do better. She could be better. Sophie has so much potential, she just needs the right person to draw it out of her – and I'm certain that person is me.

The day I first met Sophie was a turning point. Every day was the same before I met her. I knew there was something missing; I just didn't know what it was. I don't believe in all that rubbish about needing someone else to complete you or whatever. It's not like I'm a romantic kind of person. When I saw Sophie, though, it was a genuine epiphanic moment.

Sophie Portman isn't the kind of woman that would stand out in a crowd, but when we met, we weren't part of a crowd. It was just the two of us, face-to-face. She was unremarkable, in a plain black dress, and the kind of shoes that women wear to be comfortable rather than fashionable. That just added to the charm. On the surface, she's an average woman in her early thirties, but as soon as I heard her speak, I knew she was different.

"I can't believe I'm here," she said. Those were the first words I heard her speak.

"No," I replied. I already felt the shudders of attraction, and they were throwing me off-track. I wasn't sure how to continue, so I blundered, "But I'm glad you are." It was probably way too forward for our first meeting, but if we were going to spend time together and get to know each other, why not start with a confident opening?

She hadn't been looking directly at me until then, but she turned her face towards me, and gave me a wide smile that showed her orthodontic-trained teeth and made her eyes sparkle. I was gone. That's how I remember it anyway, looking back. I suppose the clichéd parts are down to the way my memory has reconstructed the moment. I want to be honest with myself, but who knows which of our memories are true and which our sad, tired brains have romanticised for us?

What I do know for sure is this: Our first conversation was awkward, but first meetings often are. There's a fine line between finding out as much as possible about someone without asking too many questions, learning about them without being too obvious about it. The skill lies in allowing the other person to do the talking. People reveal a lot more about themselves and their lives when you're not asking direct questions. All good psychiatrists know that. Probably most of the bad ones do too, but I'm not one of those.

Of course, she mentioned Jack, but she skirted around the details. It was almost as though he wasn't the main character in her life, rather he played a rather meaningless background role. One of the things about letting someone talk and listening to what they have to say, though, is that it allows you, as the observer, to take in the words and read between the lines. What someone omits to tell you can be far more important than what they actually say.

Body language can also tell you so much about how someone is thinking or feeling. It's not an exact art though. All that stuff about folding your arms and crossing your legs meaning that you're behaving defensively, sitting in an open position when you're relaxed, well, that checks out, but the less obvious details, they're more difficult to detect. One thing I did notice right from the start was that when she said Jack's name, she couldn't make eye contact. It's such a short sharp word, but each time she says it, her eyes look away, as though she's lost in some distant thought for that split second. I don't expect she's even aware that she does it. I knew, though, right at that first meeting, that something was off. I couldn't quite work out what it was, and I knew I needed to find out more details before I would really be able to unravel the truth.

Perhaps that whole thing with Jack was part of the enigma that drew me to Sophie. Perhaps it was just that I saw her as a riddle to be solved. There was a surface Sophie that she presented to the world, her professional, practical, public self, but there was also a deep layer of her that was there to be discovered. I've always been drawn to mysteries, that's essentially why I am in the job I am. Digging deep, unpicking the past, and trying to find meaning is what makes me tick. I need to understand things, but the deeper I chip away, the more fragile her exterior persona becomes. I wonder if that's what went wrong between her and Jack. Did he fracture her in some way, or was she already broken?

All I know for sure right now is that she couldn't talk about him. Not then, when we first met, and not now. This time she ran away rather than start to face the reality of their relationship. What happens next, though, and whether she is going to return, is anyone's guess. She needs her therapy sessions. If she's ever going to come to terms with the past and move on to the future, she has to come back. She has to.

CHAPTER TEN

Jack.

The last letter I wrote was abrupt. I'm sorry. I can't begin to explain the stress I am going through right now. I know you always thought I was such a calming influence on you, so reassuring and such a strong woman, but I think I may have misled you. I'm out of control, and I think I have been for some time. I tried to talk to the doctor this week, I really tried, but when he wanted me to start getting into what really happened between you and me, I had a meltdown. I couldn't do it. I'm such a disappointment; I'm disappointed in myself and I know if you were here, you'd be disappointed too.

I can tell you now, and it's quite a relief to be able to do so, that I don't think I was ever the person who you thought I was. When we met, I was not long out of a terrible relationship, and you know some of that story. I wasn't looking for a partner; you know that, too. We stumbled into our romance. Strangers to friends to sort-of lovers, and then, well, we were spending so much time together we had to make it official. For me, I must admit, part of it was that I didn't want you to be with anyone else. I was too comfortable, and per-haps too lazy, to date multiple people, but I could sense you had the potential to be quite the prolific dater.

Nothing wrong with that. We weren't together back then, not *properly*. There was no agreement we would be monogamous. While we were still on the open side of dating, you could see whom-ever you chose, but I hated the thought of it. I wanted exclusivity at the expense of sexual lib-erty, so I rushed into our relationship, pushing you before you were ready, I'm sure. When it came to it, I know I was the one pressing for marriage. I engineered and expedited our relationship so that

I wouldn't be alone, so that I had someone to love. I always thought you loved me too, at least back then I did. Once upon a time.

I thought, and I don't know why I ever let myself believe this, that once we were married, you would stop taking the overseas expeditions. I thought having a wife – and perhaps even a child – you would want to stay at home, be happy with what we had and drop the wanderlust that guided you through your adventurous single life. I thought your exciting field work abroad was part of your bachelor lifestyle, that the trips reflected something you were lacking that I could replace. I was wrong, wrong, wrong.

I was also wrong to try to change you, of course. I was wrong to *want* to change you, selfish, probably, but once we fell into the comfort of our relationship, the warm security was all I wanted. When I became Mrs Portman, and you carried on planning international field trips, I was at a loss. You were offered the Arizona trip and told me you couldn't refuse. Then came the others. New York, Barcelona, Australia. I tried to be understanding. I really did. But when the Russia job came up, and you told me how stiff the competition would be and how many other people wanted the place on the team, well, I thought it would be easy for you to refuse. You could say *no thank you*, stay at home with me, and that would be the end of it. Instead, it became your mission to be the chosen one.

Despite my feelings, I smiled, asked what I could do to help, and supported you as much as I could. It's not like I lied to you. I wanted you to be happy, and of course I wanted you to succeed, but I never wanted you to go.

There. I've finally admitted it.

I never wanted you to go.

Each person decides what parts of themselves to reveal to another, and what parts to conceal. I'm not saying that it's necessarily a conscious thing, although I accept that sometimes, of course, it is.

When we meet someone new, particularly some-body whom we wish to impress, or at least not send running, we emphasise the positive and try our absolute best not to let them see the fragments of our personalities that might be best hidden away.

That's fine when it comes to relationships, but what about when it comes to talking to my thera-pist? I know I am not opening up to him. I'm not being completely truthful about anything. I've still not told him what happened in December. How can I? Part of me thinks it's something that should remain between us. Part of me knows once I tell someone, anyone, the truth, the floodgates are going to open. I don't think I can handle the deluge that will follow.

I have to ask a question. It seems ridiculous but hear me out. I've started to believe it's you I'm seeing. It almost makes sense to my messed-up mind. When you were away before, sometimes I thought I saw you. Even though I knew, logically, it couldn't be you. Even after I had seen you on FaceTime a few hours before, sitting in a café in New York, or wherever you were that time around, even then, I sometimes imagined I had seen you. Once, I even ran up to a man in the Kwik Shop, convinced he was you. Same height, same hair, but, of course, he wasn't you. You were on the other side of the world, and I was here, waiting.

I suppose I was just missing you. I suppose I am now. No, I know I am. I can't get my head around the fact we will never be together again; it's too much to take in. Maybe that's why my brain is trying to show me that you are everywhere, you are everyone. You are watching me.

Like I said, ridiculous.

Thinking of you always.

Soph.

CHAPTER ELEVEN

When the following Tuesday morning comes
around, I'm ready. It's been a long week, and I've
thought and over thought how Sophie left the last
session. She has to start talking about Jack. I know
that; she knows that. Perhaps it was too soon to
open that line of discussion, though. If it comes
from her, if she's the one to instigate the conversation, she might not be as choked and defensive.
Without digging up the past, she's not going to be
able to bury it.

This week, even before the appointment time
of nine o'clock, I've already started to pace the
room. I should sit, settle into a comfortable, professional position, and be ready for her. Try to
think positive thoughts, manifest what I want to
happen, not what I think might happen. But I
know. My instincts tell me she's not going to turn
up.

When the hands on the clock make the right angle of the time she is due, there's no sign of Sophie. I'm sure Henny or Lola would have said something if she had cancelled, but no. Nothing. Just an empty chair.

So, what now? Call her? Check where she is? Perhaps she's running late. I'm sure she walks to the office, so it can't be the traffic. She must be spending longer getting ready for her appointments now. That must be it. Last time she was looking more together somehow, until the subject of what happened with Jack was brought up. Stupid. Maybe she had a shower first, just like I do for her. She could be straightening her hair, choosing what to wear, picking out the perfect outfit for me.

I already know, in my heart, that I'm wrong. She's not coming.

When she hasn't arrived by ten past, it's definitely time for that phone call. One side of it goes like this:

Hello. It's Doctor Thacker. Yes. No, I was worried about you. Are you running late? Did you want to reschedule? No. Well, of course I think that… Yes. Okay. No, that's completely… Whenever you're ready. Yes.

She's skipping the session. That's not a complete wash-out. It's not as though she's never going to return. She needs time, and that's fine, but she needs to carry on with her therapy. I don't even know if she picked up her meds, whether she stuck to the plan to take the antipsychotics. How stupid not to have asked her. I have to see her. I have to know.

As the phone settles back onto the receiver, the door opens and Henny bustles in, all business, no emotion.

"No show?" she asks, although the answer is patently obvious.

I try not to look at her as if she is stupid, but sometimes I have trouble hiding my emotions. It's something I need to work on. She doesn't see my expression, anyway.

"Mrs Portman is going to phone to confirm a new appointment." Pause. "Keep this slot open for her, if you can. Don't book anyone else in."

Henny raises her eyebrows at the command, and I know she's making a silent judgement. Perhaps she should try working on her professional front, too. I make a mental note to keep a closer eye on her. Even though she's my favourite assistant, she needs to stay in line. Besides, if she starts behaving like this with the patients, I'm sure Lola will follow suit. The pair of them could career out of control quite easily.

"For next week, or ongoing?" Henny's voice is arid.

"Ongoing." Straightforward, not snappy. Good. Even if she is veering off-script, there's no reason for her boss to slip into the same behaviour. "I'm sure she'll be back. We had a tough session last week. You know what it's like when they start getting into the bones of the matter."

The assistant stares as though she doesn't understand the sentence, or maybe the sentiment, but still, she nods. Henny probably has no idea what goes on between the four walls of the psychiatrist's office. She books them in, checks them out, and I don't suppose she could care less about what happens in their actual sessions.

"Ongoing, then," she complies. "More tea?" she asks, craning her head to look into the mug that's still sitting untouched where she left it nearly an hour ago.

"A top-up would be lovely." That's it. Back into the swing. No need to stress over Sophie. She'll be back. She needs this.

I almost convince myself I'm fine, that not seeing her today is a non-issue, but when Henny turns
heel and bumbles off to make fresh tea, I sink into
my chair.

Sophie will be back. She does need this. But
I'm starting to think I need it more than she does.

CHAPTER TWELVE

Jack.

I skipped my session today. I know you would be mad at me, but I couldn't face it. I set my alarm for eight, convinced myself I had every intention of attending, but part of me has known all week I wouldn't be going back this morning.

Doctor Thacker wrote me a prescription, and I've started to take the pills. That must be one point in my favour. You know I've always been against that sort of thing, but if my anxiety is causing delusions, I'd rather give drugs a try. No matter how much I don't want to take them, it's nothing compared to how much I don't want to talk about December.

I've felt this increasing sense of dread since the last session. I'm not sure how I can talk about losing you when I still feel you here with me. I don't think talking about what happened would do any good. It's not going to change anything.

I know it was my fault. I wanted you to stay with me, and all I did was push you away. I didn't want you to leave, and I ruined everything. How can I tell anyone what I did when I can't make peace with it in my own head?

When I think back over the past few years, I can't work out where we started to go wrong, and I definitely don't know why. If I could calculate the exact date and time, it wouldn't matter anyway. It's not like we can go back and do it all again, take a different path and do it right next time. Life doesn't work that way. All I have is the here and now, on my own. As for the future, well, who knows what that will bring?

Nothing good. Nothing good is going to happen because I don't deserve it.

Remember last time I wrote, I said I thought it might be you that was watching me? When I first started to feel that way, it was a scary thought. How could you be? You're not at home with me now; you're not with me anymore. The more I thought about it, though, the more I started to like the idea. If this is all in my head, which I hope to hell it is, then who would I rather be watching me than you?

You always said you'd never leave me, and all the times you went away, no matter how far from me you seemed, or how long the weeks felt, you always came back to me. Maybe if I hold on to the thought it could be you, well, maybe then I won't have to accept the truth.

You won't leave me. You can't leave me. But I know you're never coming back to our life here.

I keep writing these letters as if one day you're going to be able to read them, but when I sign my name on the bottom and slide them into their sleek white envelopes all I do is put them into the drawer on your side of the bed. You still have a side of the bed. I sometimes roll over in the night and reach my arm across to bring you towards me, assume the big spoon position you always preferred me to take, and snuggle my face against the warm, musky skin of your back. Of course, you're not here, and it's me, alone, with only a pillow to embrace.

If I am seeing you, it's not a bad thing. I'm sorry for what I did, but I can't change it. And I certainly can't talk about it.

Sophie

CHAPTER THIRTEEN

Even though Sophie missed her appointment, Jonah the faithful puppy turns up at bang on nine o'clock on Thursday morning. Neither of us are happy about it, but these sessions are a means to an end. One of us gets money, and the other gets, well, I'm not quite sure. Better? That's how Sophie would put it.

There's no dawdling in the waiting room today, trying to chat up the assistants or cadging a cup of tea before the appointment. It's straight in the building and straight into the room.

"You seem distant today."

"It's been a hard week."

"Hard? Do you want to tell me about that?"

"No."

Rookie mistake number one. Don't ask closed questions. All they do is give the patient the opportunity to shut the conversation down. Much better to ask something open as an invitation to spill their guts.

I look at him and feel the heart sink that comes with knowing I'm here for the rest of the hour.

"Okay. I've had too much time on my own. It's been quiet at work and –"

"Work?"

Another error. Don't interrupt the patient when they're talking. Not unless it's essential, anyway. Which this isn't.

"Yeah. Anyway, I'm used to always having something to do. When there's a lull, it gives me more time to think. The more time I have to think, the more likely I am to think about the things I don't want to think about. I mean, I do want to think about them, but you don't want me to, er, I don't…"

The words loop around, and there doesn't seem to be an end to this chain of thought. An interruption is acceptable this time. There's probably something in the textbooks that says if your patient starts hyperventilating and looking like they're about to have a panic attack, you're perfectly within your rights to help them.

"Alright, alright."

"I'm fine, it's okay."

I hold out my hand, and the two of us stand between our chairs for a moment, like partners, inviting each other to dance. Not here, though. No thank you. Not today. Instead, I slowly sit back down, and he does the same, practically mirroring my gestures. That means something. Mimicry isn't to do with mocking someone, it's a subconscious way to show empathy. Skilled therapists can make this a conscious gesture, copying their patients' movements to make them feel more secure, better understood. Therapy is all about other people's lies and the lies you can make them believe in the name of helping them.

When we have both settled down, I give him a few moments of breathing space. Meanwhile, I can't help but cast my eyes over him, looking for signs of his state of mind, but also trying to figure out this man that I sit with for an hour every week. We've been having these sessions for more or less the same length of time Sophie has been having her sessions. The difference is I already feel like I know so much about her, the way she thinks, her mannerisms and actions. I know barely anything about the man in front of me, and I'm very much aware I'm to blame for that. I should keep my focus, try to put everything I can into these appointments. But the truth is, I'm bored. Still, we carry on.

"So, Jonah. What have you been thinking about?"

Thinking about; obsessing over. You say po-tay-ato, I say po-tah-to. Does it matter what we call it at this point? As long as we're working through it, the end result should be the same.

"I was *thinking about* her. I was thinking she's to blame for all this."

She. Her. Those words can only remind me of Sophie. I might not see her next week; I may never see her again. I feel a throbbing in my hands, and it's only when I look down that I see I've balled my hands into fists and I'm gripping them tightly enough to turn my knuckles white.

I can't be like this. Not here, not now. Not in front of him.

"I, er, we can't blame other people for our own thoughts and feelings. No matter how malicious other people may be, we need to remember we are in control of our own responses. If someone does something we find offensive or hurtful, it's up to us to process that action and consider how we want to react."

It sounds like therapy mumbo jumbo, but I have to keep us both on track.

"She left me. She rejected me. After everything we went through, after all the promises we made to each other. We were meant to be together."

I rub my hand thoughtfully over my face as I listen to the clichés fall to the ground. All remarkably interesting, and nothing to do with Sophie. Good. Let's move forward with this, then.

"We can explore this further if you feel it would be helpful."

"I was fine. I wasn't like this when we were together, but then, when she met him, everything fell apart. I'm not good enough. I wasn't good enough then and I'm not good enough now and I have no idea how to change that. I might as well not be here. I'm wasting your time. You're never going to help me."

"I'm trained to help you. That's what you are here for. All you have to do is come along, be honest and open, and commit to making positive change."

Maybe it *is* all mumbo jumbo. Replace the psychiatrist with a robot, sit him in the chair and get him to earn the overpriced hourly rate instead.

Having a robot listen to Jonah talk about his complex little life would be better for everyone.

The thing with therapy is that the patient has to want to get better. They have to be capable of change. Believe me, most people are, but some, well, they are so stuck in the past that they can't work through it. They can't face up to the things they have done, so there's no way they can move forwards. The skill is in leading them down the correct path, setting them off on a journey in the right direction. I look at the man in front of me, and I wonder how that is ever going to happen.

CHAPTER FOURTEEN

My Thursday morning session set the tone for the rest of my day, and by six o'clock I'm spent. I know I should cook something decent for dinner, but my mind is full of the past few hours and it's all I can do to avoid sliding open my phone and ordering Deliveroo. I'm not going to do it. Not this time. A bargain bucket from *Cluckin' Joes* may seem like a great option, but the delivery driver visits my home so often I'm thinking about asking him to start paying rent. When I start to smile at my own stupid joke, I know it's time to drag my lazy butt out of the chair and go out like a man and hunt for my dinner. In a manner of speaking, of course.

My go-to hunting ground is the Kwik Shop, one of those hybrid stores you see in most small towns now. The shelves are packed with one or two of every item you could imagine, and there's a small booth in the back corner that functions as a post office three days a week. The central office in the town centre shut down about a year ago, along with most of the other shops I used to enjoy browsing around, so the Kwik Shop is about all that's left. I know online shopping is meant to be The Future, whatever that means, but there's something about walking around a store, picking up the products on the shelves and spending time deciding what you want that is so much more satisfying than filling an online basket and waiting days for your order to arrive. Besides, apart from what happens in the office, going to the shop is about all the social life I have. Leaving the house and wandering up and down the aisles gives me time to people-watch, and sometimes, rarely, I stop for a few minutes to have a chat with whoever's turn it is to man the till.

Today it's Jayden. He's got his head turned down towards his phone as I walk in. I can't hear what he's watching, but I just about catch sight of a video game character I recognise from the nineties.

"Hey." I make the customary greeting, but he doesn't look up. At least he has the decency to keep the sound muted.

"Hello to you too," I mutter, replying on his behalf as I shuffle towards the groceries.

He's a good kid, really. Some days, we actually have a decent chat. He works here two or three times a week, depending on college work, always the evening shift, and apart from the owner, he's the only person who's trusted to run the place alone.

For a small shop, there's a decent amount of choice, but I already know I don't have the energy to make anything exciting tonight. I'm not the greatest of cooks. Add that to the list of qualities I lack. The first aisle is the home of tinned vegetables, various jars, and an array of soups. My eyes scan over the pale-labelled cans. Potato and leek.

Pea and ham. Mushroom. All the creamy mono-tone cans of slush. Hearty soups, slim soups, blah blah blah. I'm about to reach out for a lobster bisque, twice the price as any of the other options, but alluringly exotic, when my attention is inexplicably jolted away.

There's a flash of movement as someone else walks into the aisle, her head down, looking at her phone screen as she shuffles forwards. I know before I see her face. She's wearing that dark rose cotton jacket that screams, '*look at me!*' and I can't stop myself from complying. Her hair is tucked under the collar, like she threw on her coat in a hurry. I like to take in these details, make the connections between the act and the motive, the what and the why.

I want to walk over, place my hand on her arm, give her a smile and start a conversation, but I know I can't. In the first session of therapy, where we weigh each other up and try to find a foundation to build upon, there's a laying of ground

113

rules. One of them is that if the psychiatrist and the patient meet outside of the office environment, they won't acknowledge each other. On one hand, it avoids any awkward questions. Imagine you're about to pay for your extra hot, extra shot latte and a sugar-free caramel soy whatever with your date and suddenly you're face-to-face with the man you spill your heart out to for £120 every week.

Hi, how are you doing?

Try explaining that one to your one true love. If we somehow happen to end up in the same artisan coffee house, which I very much doubt, the agreement is that we should both act as though the other person doesn't exist. No need for explanation, no embarrassing exchanges.

There's also that whole idea of everything we say being 'on the record'. How would it go if one of us asked a seemingly innocent question, and we ended up tumbling down a rabbit hole of complicated conversation?

Oh, pretty awful. I'm on a crappy date and I think I'm only seeing this girl to boost my self-confidence, but that's not working. I feel terrible.

Hold that thought until our next appointment. I'll need to bill you for that one.

Besides, we live in a small town. People know each other and have that over-friendly habit of gossiping and griping about everyone else. If Mrs Bradley from down the road or one of Kayleigh and Gayle's gang saw the two of us chatting, you could bet everyone else in town would know about it before long. I made those names up, but those types of people are everywhere, sticking their noses into other people's lives.

Anyway, if we see each other outside of the faux-domestic confines of the office, the rules are clear. Still, I hadn't prepared myself for how I was going to act should I happen to bump into Sophie. This isn't her part of town, this certainly isn't the closest shop to where she lives, and yet here she is, twenty-five feet away from me and getting closer.

Breathe slowly, calm down, and turn around, I tell myself. Casual. Careful.

Instead, I make a jab towards the shelf to pick up a can and fumble, almost knocking it to the floor. Sophie's pre-occupation with her phone has stopped her from seeing me so far, but if I stand here much longer, she's going to notice. I'm not prepared for this, and I don't think I could bear an awkward confrontation.

I'm trying my best to remain steady as I place the can into my basket, but a rush of adrenaline surges through me. I don't want to ignore her. I want to talk to her. I want more.

As soon as that thought enters my head, I know I have to leave as quickly as possible. I can't approach her. I can't even smile at her. All I could do would be to let her walk past me. I can't risk this getting out of hand. I have to stop it now. I have to stop myself.

She turns her head slightly and I hear her sharp intake of breath. I can almost sense the anxiety in her movement. There's a visible tension to her body as she jerks her head in my direction.

I turn and step around the end of the aisle, avoiding her glance. Past the display of assorted breakfast cereals and between the next shelves. I tuck myself into the corner amongst the pet food and bags of kitty litter. The rows of cat eyes look out at me in unison, and I try not to meet their gaze. Sophie doesn't have a pet; there's no reason for her to come to this part of the shop.

Above me there's a mirror that the shop's owner has set up to keep an eye on the more light-fingered of his clientele. I glance up and see Sophie hurrying towards the till.

She stumbles slightly as she approaches Jayden, and the can she's holding slips from her fingers and rolls along the floor, almost as though it is trying to make its way towards me, conspiring to give me away. As she spins on her heel to retrieve it, she looks up, and I crouch, suddenly enthralled by the six-pack of Fido chow on the bottom shelf. My heart thuds, and I wait, unable to check whether she's seen me, whether she is going to walk over.

I'm immensely relieved when I hear her talking to Jayden. Until I hear what she has to say.

"Hey, sorry. Did you… this is going to sound strange, I know, but did you see anyone following me? Was there a man…? Was someone…?"

I can imagine Jayden's professional smile. He may lack focus, but when he's talking to a customer, he does give one hundred per cent. He knows how to turn it on.

"Sorry, ma'am," he says. Not yes, not no, just an apology. "I, er…"

He was still watching his video, that's what. I could tell her that if I wasn't hiding in the pet section. If I wasn't trying to avoid her at all costs.

"You didn't see anyone?"

I glance up at the mirror from my position, squatting on the floor. I can't see her face. Her back is towards me, and I'm hemmed into this corner.

I see Jayden though, with his awkward grin, and absence of useful information. I take a tin off the shelf to study, trying to blend in as a friendly neighbourhood pet-owner. Nothing to see here. If he looks up at the security mirror, he's not going to see anything interesting.

"But you... I..." I can still hear Sophie, trying to find her words. She has that same quiet tone, filled with self-doubt and apprehension, that she does when she's in the office.

Jayden makes an apologetic grunt.

"Okay," Sophie says. Her voice is still shaky and uncertain, but she doesn't push the young shop worker further. "I'll just take this, I suppose."

There's a beep of the till as Jayden scans whatever she grabbed on impulse, and a second, quieter sound as she swipes her debit card.

"Thank you," she says.

"Sure," Jayden replies, and then, remembering where he is, "Have a good evening."

Sophie doesn't respond, and when I look up, she has gone.

I feel obliged to pick up a can of mackerel flavoured cat treats after standing in the pet section for so long, and after a considered few minutes I make my way to the till.

"Two-sixty," Jayden says, clearly unhappy about having to pause his video again to do his job.

"No problem." I hand over the correct change, not wanting to inconvenience him further, not wanting to cause any problems, not wanting to stand out.

I wonder, for a moment, if he is going to mention the woman who was here before me, but if she made any kind of impression on him, he doesn't let it show. As soon as I've paid, his eyes are back on his screen, his finger reaching out to press the triangle to resume the clip.

The chill evening air hits my face as I leave the store. I slide the can of soup into my pocket, throw the cat treats into the bin, and make my way home.

CHAPTER FIFTEEN

Jack.

You were there today in the supermarket. Or at least, that's what I'm choosing to believe. Walking alone into the places we once walked together, knowing you'll never walk with me again, never gets any easier.

There was just that young kid at the counter, you know, the one you always joked was going to end up as a cyber millionaire, and one bloke looking at cat food. Anyone who has a cat can't be a bad guy.

Thacker was right, you know. Nobody has a good reason to be watching me. My life, especially now you aren't here, is barely interesting enough for me, never mind anyone else.

The only thing that makes sense is that I am seeing you. My mind is tricking me into thinking you're around because it's what I want to believe.

You told me once about something called Occam's razor: the simplest explanation is most likely to be true. Sure, some random stranger might have decided I'm fascinating enough that he wants to spend his life observing me, or hey, it could be an alien life form that's waiting for the right moment to abduct me. That wouldn't even seem like a bad fate some days. My point is this: the simplest explanation is that what happened back in December triggered a breakdown, and now I am seeing you everywhere.

You're never coming back, so if the only way I can see you is in my head, then perhaps I should be hanging onto that, rather than trying to be cured. If the drugs start to make a difference, maybe I won't see you anymore. Maybe not being watched will feel worse. If seeing your ghost, or even the flicker of it, is all I have left, perhaps I shouldn't try to get rid of it. I can't bear to think about letting go.

Stay with me.

Soph

CHAPTER SIXTEEN

Ever since we almost ran into each other, I've been wondering whether Sophie saw me, and whether she's going to say anything. I say *'wondering'*, but I mean obsessing. The thought has occupied too much of my time and energy, and I've had to make a conscious effort to focus on other things to take my mind off it. I wonder sometimes how I ended up like this, how one woman has the power to turn me from a reasonable, logical, generally intelligent man into an obsessive idiot. She's a very special woman, though.

To the outside world, Sophie Portman may appear average, but once you start to unravel her, she's a fascinating person. The way she thinks, the things she does. I don't even know where to start. It wasn't her looks that first drew me to her, but she is undeniably appealing.

Attraction is a complex affair. There's no universal law that governs it. There are no rules for how or why we are drawn to other people. Sometimes these temptations happen against our better judgement, despite factors or situations that should stand in the way.

Sophie. A psychiatric patient. A married woman. Sophie. Sophie. Sophie. Does it still count as being married now Jack is gone? For now, I suppose it does.

Of course, I have always known it's impossible for her and me to connect in the ways I would like us to. I've thought it through so many times, run through so many scenarios, trying to work out a way she and I could be together, but I know it's impossible. That doesn't stop me from feeling the way I do. In fact, in some ways, it makes the feelings stronger. We always want what we cannot have. The unattainable is eminently more attrac-

126

tive than the easily obtained. Would I be so attracted to her if our relationship could become a reality? Probably. Possibly.

I'm lost in my thoughts when I hear the familiar triple tap on the door. It's her. She's arrived.

When Sophie walks into the room, I take a few moments to compose myself, straighten my posture, and focus my attention. It's so easy to get caught up in my thoughts sometimes. This hour is Sophie's, not mine, and my concentration should be completely upon her. After her missed week, I'm hungry for her presence, and it takes more effort than usual for me to relax.

We're almost into August now, and the temperature outside has risen to an almost uncomfortable twenty-eight degrees, so warm that Sophie has foregone her ubiquitous pink jacket. She's dressed in a smart but casual dress - a navy-coloured jersey-type fabric that hangs loosely over her curves. A blue and white floral headband

127

perches crown-like upon her head, her fringe hanging below it.

"Sophie. Good morning."

It is a good morning. Every morning that I see Sophie is a good morning.

"Hi," she says. "Warm, isn't it?"

My room is stuffy and heavy with heat. I already feel sticky and listless, and I've only been sitting in this chair for ten minutes. She's not paying to talk about the temperature, though. If she finds some random, meaningless topic to talk about, she probably thinks she can avoid explaining why she didn't show last time. We both know, though. It seems pointless to alienate her by dragging it up.

Move onwards.

"How have you been since I last saw you?"

A dainty shrug. "Same old," she says.

It's a common stereotype that British people answer the question '*how are you?*' with '*fine*' or '*okay thanks*' when those responses are actually

128

far from the truth. There's something about the stiff-upper-lip attitude or the stoic front that makes it easier to disguise true feelings behind platitudes or weasel words. And sure, that is *fine* – to some extent – when you're chatting to a casual acquaintance or colleague, but when it comes to discussing your mental health with your therapist, these euphemisms don't quite cut it.

"I'm glad you've come back." I really am. "Tell me what's been happening."

Let's get straight to the point, deep into the good stuff. But then, as soon as I think this, she speaks, and I immediately regret it.

"In the supermarket last week…" she begins.

My heart almost stops. I feel myself moving forwards in my seat, sitting to attention, and have to will myself to hold back, to relax down into the chair again.

"What happened?"

She places her hands softly on her lap. I notice she's painted her nails since she was last in the office. Instead of the chipped varnish, there's a fresh coat of coral coloured gloss. I wonder if it means anything but thinking about it doesn't calm me.

"Nothing," she says. "I'm sure it was nothing."

But of course, she wouldn't have mentioned it if it was nothing, so all I can do is sit through the gap in conversation while she shuffles slightly and decides what to say. I observe her face, trying to gauge her expression, trying to get a read on her emotion. She's biting her lip, only slightly, but enough so I can see it. I don't know what it means. I don't know how to decode her.

"I may as well tell you, now I've brought it up." It's almost as though she is dangling a carrot, leading me forward. I should be in control, not her. She shifts a little in her chair, her eyes scanning the room, looking to the window, half-shuttered, before returning her attention. "The Kwik Shop, down the road here. I stopped in on a whim really, not for anything special, you know."

I know. I know too well.

"I wasn't concentrating, so that's why I'm not sure. I was… anyway… I just had the feeling again there someone was watching me. Down the next aisle or, I don't know, between the shelves. You can't even see between the shelves. That's why it's so stupid. There couldn't have been anyone. The place was pretty dead."

She shakes her head and stops speaking.

"Were there staff in the shop? Did anybody see anything? Or anyone?"

I know the answer before she speaks. I've been back to the Kwik Shop, on more than one occasion, since Thursday. I spoke to Jayden, making sure he hadn't picked up on anything unusual or out of the ordinary, but his head was back on his phone screen. Say what you will about modern technology, but it certainly has its uses.

"No," she confirms. "Ridiculous."

"Ridiculous?"

"Ridiculous," she repeats. "I know you're trying to help me to see this is all in my head, but I don't know. For some reason, I still keep seeing him everywhere." She pauses, and then, in a timid whisper, she says, "I thought it was him. I thought it was Jack." Before there's any time for a response, she lets out a short, sharp laugh, as if her brain is acknowledging how *ridiculous* her thoughts sound.

"Jack? You mean you thought it was him watching you? But Jack…"

Jack is gone.

Jack is lost.

Jack isn't around anymore.

"Like I said, ridiculous."

Sophie shakes her head again slowly, and one slow tear slides down her cheek. My impulse is to lean forward, wipe it away, offer a hug, but of course I can't do that.

"I want to believe that it's him, that one day he'll be back," she stutters. "But it can't be, and he won't be."

This is it, I think, *this is when she starts to talk.*

Instead, she fumbles in her pocket for a tissue and wipes away the tear.

"I'm sorry," she says.

The wet smudge of her mascara on the white paper reminds me of those tests that reveal the inner workings of the psyche or whatever. You might see a face or a bat or, if your mind has the tendency, something sexual. When I look at it, all I see is blackness.

"Can we talk about Jack?" she asks, and then, more firmly, "I need to talk about Jack."

It's about time. It's taken all these sessions for her to be ready, but at last, she's come to this on her own. I knew she would, eventually, she just needed time. I feel the trace of a smile form on my lips and snap it back.

"If you're ready. Of course."

133

"I don't really know where to start. Maybe I can tell you about him. Can we start there?" She doesn't wait for an answer. Instead, she races ahead. "He's a geologist. I wish I could tell you more about what he does, but…"

She shifts in her seat and then, as though aware of her fidgeting, and wishing to put a stop to it she settles her flat pumps firmly against the floor and places her hands into her lap.

"He'd start to explain, and I wanted to look as though I understood what he was talking about but…" She shrugs and raises her hands. "Mostly I had no idea. The Arkhangelsk trip though, it was a big deal. I understood that much."

She whoops a deep, loud inhalation.

"I never wanted him to go, you know. I told him; I mean I didn't want to stop him from *'following his dream'*." She forms quotation marks in the air with her fingers.

In return I nod, acknowledging the words. Despite what she says, her voice is heavy with guilt.

I'm almost holding my breath waiting to find out how much she is going to say. She can't just want to talk about him in this general, vague sense. Surely bringing this conversation to the room means she's ready to address what happened.

"Can you tell me more about what happened?"

She must have known it was coming, but the look on her face is one of surprise and disorientation.

"What I think happened?" she asks but doesn't wait for a reply, "Or what I am afraid happened?"

Again, she shakes her head. "The last time base station saw him, he was setting out on a routine data collection trip. Just another ordinary day. That's what gets me, you know, everything was the same as any other day. All those trivial things we take for granted, running through daily routines and chores, and then..."

"What?"

"No radio contact, nothing. It was almost as though he was wiped off the face of the Earth. There were two others on the team, Jane and Caroline. Both of them did what they could. They looked around the area he was meant to be working in, but there was no sign he had even made it to the site."

She sounds incredibly matter of fact about providing this information. It's hard to believe she is telling the story about how her husband apparently vanished.

"So, Jack has been gone for…"

"Seven months. Seven months, two weeks, and four days."

A slow, silent nod. Compassion. A show of understanding. Of course, you can never really understand how someone else feels. You can develop empathy and insight, but each person's own feelings are just that - their own. How I experience the loss of a loved one isn't necessarily the same as how someone else would. Sophie's pain is her own.

"Seven months." The words echoed back to the patient, give them the opportunity to respond, invite them to say more without trying to fill in the gaps with one's own feelings. Everything has to come from her. This is her chance to open up.

Instead of speaking further though, the tears she hasn't yet shown during her sessions finally form. Holding back is never a clever idea, not in sessions like this. That's not what therapy is for. To really get the most out of it, patients have to let go, be honest, reveal everything, and truly bare their souls.

Sophie hasn't got up and left, there's no running away this time, so I know that she is going to face up to the truth, eventually. It's all a matter of when. She's ready to talk, but apparently she's not ready to say anything important.

Still, she lets out a sigh, with a broad smile on her face, as though she is proud of what she's achieved.

"Well done, Sophie. It must have been tough for you to talk me through that."

She nods, keeping that smile beaming out.

"I don't expect I'm cured now," she says. "But at least I'm talking, right? That's got to help."

Always looking for approval. Always wanting to know she's saying the right thing. Sophie is so transparent sometimes. Not necessarily hungry for attention, but for the conformation that she's not messing everything up. I'm sure she wants to come across as a regular, normal person. I'm also fairly certain she's not the kind of woman who would have told anyone that they are attending therapy.

"The more we can talk through your thoughts and feeling and work through them together, the more progress we will be able to make."

"Thank you," she says. "I want to talk, I really do."

I want to believe her, but when I look at her sitting there, smiling as though she has worked through all of her issues in this one session, I have to doubt her. Talking is no good unless you're ready to tell the truth.

CHAPTER SEVENTEEN

I work until five, and when I get home, I can almost smell the emptiness of my home. Sometimes I feel like a fish in a tank that's too big for him. That's better than the alternative, but it makes me so conscious I am alone, and the place I live in was bought by a couple, for a couple.

Serena and I weren't planning to start a family or anything, but the flat is big enough to accommodate an extra small person if we had ever gone down that avenue. Instead, there were potholes, street repairs, and eventually the metaphorical road was closed. The room that could have been a nursery is now a study, but being in there brings back too many jagged memories for me to put it to any use.

I could sell up, move out and move on, but despite the memories that float around me here, I like the place. It was me that chose it, not Serena.

She wasn't that interested in where we lived, or what the property was like. Either she trusted my judgement, or she had already started to do her own kind of looking around, even then. Nothing would surprise me.

I researched everything, of course, because that's what I do. I want to know every detail whenever I make any kind of weighty decision. What are the neighbours like? What's the crime rate? What does OFSTED say about the local schools? Not that we ever needed that information. I even looked into the public transport services; despite the fact I would never take a bus. I hate the feel of dirty seats beneath me and dirty people beside me. The sound of strangers chatting to each other in public makes me bristle. Some people have an irrational dislike of hearing other people eating, I just have a dislike of hearing other people. In public, anyway. If I have the choice between catching a bus or walking, I'll take the second option. Dirty, dirty people.

My interest in other people's lives is limited to those I have to talk to for work. Meeting Serena, getting to know her, building a relationship was mentally and emotionally challenging. Sophie, on the other hand, is easy. She is easy to be with, easy to talk to, easy on the eye. Everything about her, no matter how complicated she might think she is, is easy. Perhaps that's her real appeal.

It was never like that with Serena. It took me eighteen months to ask Serena out for dinner, and even then, she didn't realise it was a date. We saw each other nearly every day, and I tried to make conversation, even though I can't stand small talk. I inconvenienced myself to get to know her, and gradually, she warmed to me. Or at least I thought she did.

I invited her for dinner at the Thai restaurant near the office. It was the best I could think of. I wanted her to see that I wasn't a fast-food lowlife. I needed to impress her.

At the end of the night, I leaned towards her in that awkward, stumbling way that seems to be the norm for a first date, and she actually laughed. Not a booming *that-was-hilarious* kind of laugh, but a sniffed chuckle. She hadn't expected it, and I didn't realise that until I was moving towards her lips.

It wasn't even as if she pulled away. She froze, her eyes locked on mine, and covered her mouth with her hand.

Thinking she was putting a physical blocker to the kiss, I drew back, almost tripping against the wall behind me.

Serena shook her head and moved her hand away to show a smile.

"It's okay," she said. "I didn't realise. I'm stupid. I'm sorry."

"I shouldn't have…" I began to say, but she interrupted, putting the hand that had just rested on her lips, onto my hand.

"Shh," she said. "It's okay."

I wondered then if she could sense my inexperience and nervousness, and whether that would turn her off, or maybe even turn her on. I thought I knew her so well, but at that moment I realised I didn't know her at all.

Of course, we kissed. She leaned up, pulled me down, and I'm sure I don't have to describe how kisses happen. We kissed.

For a while, that's all that happened between us. We went on dates, we kissed, and I dreamed of being a more confident, assertive person. We stumbled into a relationship, and gradually, I built a life around Serena. Our relationship was all that mattered to me; I would have done anything for her, and I did.

And that is how I ended up here.

How I ended up on my own is a different story; it's a story that I can't face thinking about tonight. I had Serena and now she is gone. When I have Sophie, I'm never going to let her go. I'll never make that mistake again.

CHAPTER EIGHTEEN

Jack.

You know I never wanted you to go. Somehow, this didn't seem the same as all the other trips. Barcelona, Arizona, even that month you spent in New South Wales. At least you could phone me. It wasn't like we were completely apart.

Do you remember the night you told me? You came in home so excited, champagne in hand – real champagne, not the cheap type your mother always pulls out at Christmas. I know you'd give me that look if you were here, but you're not, so I can say it, can't I?

School had been hectic that day. It was open evening again, my least favourite time of the year, when I had to work from half-past eight in the morning until half-past nine at night, keeping a smile on my face for prospective students and their doting, over-enthusiastic parents. At least history is a straightforward topic to talk about. I didn't have to set up experiments or complicated lab displays like some of the teachers. I did, however, have to stand to attention and schmooze all the visitors on an empty stomach and with aching feet.

By the time I got home, all I wanted to do was run a bath and soak away the stresses of the day. My legs were numb, and the cloudy aura of a migraine was starting to creep behind my left eye. I called your name as I walked through the door, but you didn't reply. It must have been nearly ten by then, but I thought maybe you'd gone for drinks with your oh-so-wonderful team.

It wasn't until I was about to step into the bath that I heard you at the door. Not just the rattling fumble I was so used to, but I could hear that you were calling me. Even before you got into the hallway, you were shouting my name.

Sophie! Soph!

146

Like a kid who got what they wanted for Christmas.

Soph!

I caught my reflection in the not-quite-steamed-up mirror. I remember my expression. I knew what was coming.

I'd already stripped off my top, and I was standing there in my skirt and bra. It felt almost comedic. I wasn't going to carry on undressing, but there was no point stripping further. All I could do was to wait.

Sophie!

You came into the house, and I heard you make your way into the living room

Soph!

and kitchen

Sophie, where are you? Soph.

I could have locked the bathroom door, locked myself in, and locked you out. I could have hidden from the truth for longer, delayed the moment, but

I knew it was coming, and I knew there was no escape.

You had waited for days to find out whether you were going to be chosen for the expedition, and your excited voice could only mean one thing. I knew you were going away again. You were leaving me, and I would be facing Christmas alone.

Sophie!

You came up the stairs, two at a time, leaping towards me like a salmon up a stream. Only you weren't returning to your home ground. You were coming to tell me you were leaving.

I must sound like a sour old cow. I should have been thrilled you had got the posting. There were two or three others – more you told me – in your department, just as eager as you, and probably just as skilled. You'd be the first to admit you aren't the leader in your field. I knew how much it meant to you, though. Arkhangelsk. The Arctic Circle.

Even the name sounds enchanting, exotic, and wild.

Not for the first time, you were happy, and I knew I wasn't the reason.

When you pushed open the bathroom door, eyes wide, arms open, repeating my name, I couldn't help but to let you embrace me. The champagne bottle pressed against the warm skin of my back, and you whispered softly into my ear.

"I'm going to Arkhangelsk, Soph. They picked me."

You had got what you wanted for Christmas, after all.

And me? Well, you and I know what happened next.

Soph

CHAPTER NINETEEN

I listen to Henny and Lola chatting about their planned summer holidays for a full fifteen minutes while I wait for Sophie to arrive. I was up early and ready for the appointment. The excitement of seeing her helps me to get out of bed in the morning. Isn't that what love should be like?

Again, she's late. It's becoming such a common occurrence that I don't even worry she is going to skip her session again. It's almost as though somehow, I would *know* if she wasn't going to come.

I barely have time to think about what I'll do if she doesn't turn up when I hear that tap-tap-tap on the door, and in she walks.

"Good morning, Sophie."

It seems smiling is too much effort for her today.

"Hi," she says, flat and business-like.

This is almost a *pull my chair forward and lean in for a close-up* moment, but I restrain myself and try to remain relaxed.

"I didn't want to come today," she says, crossing her arms defensively.

I know that I said interpreting body language isn't an exact art, but it's perfectly clear she's putting up a barrier.

"No?"

I doubt she's going to say the reason she didn't want to come is that she is feeling so much better now, thank you very much.

"No." She sighs an exaggerated breathy sigh and continues. "The drugs aren't helping. These sessions aren't helping. All I do is sit at home and watch myself going crazy. I don't want to go out. Everywhere I go, I see him, and I can't handle it anymore."

"It takes a little while for the antipsychotics to kick in…"

"Psychotic? Is that what I am now?"

151

Well, that was clearly the wrong word to use.

"Technically, that's the name for your medication. We are trying to treat your anxiety and depression, and eradicate, er, get rid of these delusions. Stop you from seeing things."

"You don't have to explain things to me as if I'm stupid," she snaps. "I'm an educated woman, you know. Even if I am psychotic."

"Sophie, calm down, please."

Telling a psychiatric patient to calm down when you're the one that's just wound them up in the first place is also not particularly a desirable avenue to go down.

"Sure, okay, fine. I am calm. I'm just not sure what I'm doing here anymore. Nothing seems to change as a result of it."

"What do you want to change?"

"Well, do you remember I asked you how long it would take for me to get better?"

Nod.

"I want to start getting better. I want to see some progress. I want to feel like I'm getting some value for my money."

She immediately raises her right hand.

"I don't mean that. It's not about the money. I just want things to change."

Nod. Nod again.

"Last time you seemed so much more positive. Has something happened?"

"Nothing has happened. Nothing ever happens."

I thought that after last week we were getting somewhere. She seemed so proud of herself when she left, even though it was probably unjustified. Perhaps this is a way to avoid digging deeper. She could be trying to cause a disturbance so she doesn't have to go into any more details about Jack. Let's leave that for now. Change direction, or rather, establish a direction.

"How about we start setting some goals, so you can work towards them? Small steps, nothing major. You might feel like you're making progress if you set some goals and achieve them?" A question, more than a statement.

Come on, we're in this together, Sophie.

A quick flick of the eyebrows makes me believe that she's sceptical, but still she says, "Okay. Like what?"

"Well, you said you're sitting at home watching yourself go crazy."

Always try to use the patient's own words. It shows you've been listening. It's one of the best ways to demonstrate your empathy. Making a patient feel like they are being heard can have a positive effect on the sessions. Or so it says in the books. Sometimes it appears more like going through the motions.

"How about we think of a plan that will help you to stop feeling like that?"

"That would be a start," she says, almost managing a smile.

"Okay, well, what do you do with your time, Sophie?"

Her face is blank.

"What do you get up to at home? It's been seven months. How are you keeping yourself occupied?"

"Well, I come here once a week," she says, forcing a smile

I'd like to smile too, but it's more sad than it is funny.

"Apart from that?"

"Not much," she says, her voice softer. "I spend a bit of time in the garden."

She pauses for a few moments, but I can tell she has more to say. I wait.

"I stopped going out. I mean, I wasn't one for socialising anyway, not really. When I started to get these feelings though, that I was being watched, I wanted to stay at home, hide away, I suppose."

"Feelings that you were being watched."

Repeating back the patient's words, emphasising their phrasing back to them, is meant to reaffirm or validate their beliefs. I got that from the books too.

"Yes," she says. "Feelings. Whether what I am feeling is real, it made me not want to go out anymore. But I know where you're going with this. I have so much time on my hands that I sit at home worrying about what I'm feeling, letting my imagination run wild."

"Is that what's happening?"

"Maybe. Possibly," she concedes.

"This might seem like a huge step, but I have a suggestion for you. Don't jump to an answer straight away. You're going to need to think about this." Dramatic pause for effect. "How would you feel about going back to work?"

She looks so taken aback she might as well have been asked how she'd feel about cutting off her arm.

"Work? I... well, I don't... I haven't... I haven't really spent that much time with other people. Not since..."

"I know that it's not going to be the same. You had friends there, though?"

She shrugs, a simple, slight rise and fall of her shoulders.

"Colleagues then? People you didn't mind spending your time with?"

"I keep myself to myself mostly," she says. "I'm not great at making conversation. I've never really been interested in other people's lives. I taught my classes, got on with my work and hid away in my office when it was time for a break."

We have so much in common. The more she talks, the more I see it.

"No staff wild nights out? No drinks in town with the girls?"

157

I catch a look that she quickly disguises.

"Not even when Jack was away. When he was home, I wanted to get back from work to him as soon as I could. When he was away, well, I don't know. I suppose I've never been into that whole thing. I was never all that social."

She leans back in her chair, and I can almost sense the avalanche of words that are about to fall from her mouth.

"I tried. Maybe not all that hard, maybe not hard enough. I wasn't popular at school, always on the edge, never part of the cool gang, so when I got to college I really tried. It was a chance to reinvent myself, to move away from the Sophie that the kids at my school had known and ignored. I talked my mum into buying me some clothes I thought were trendy, the kind of uniform that would make me fit in with the students in the cliques. I learnt how to straighten my hair, slap on the makeup, make myself look like one of them.

That was all surface, though. When it came down to it, I was the same stupid Sophie."

Suddenly seeming self-conscious, she stops, mid-tirade.

"I was still a socially awkward idiot. There was no changing that. I skirted around the edges of groups, trying to find an in. Until I decided I wasn't bothered anymore. I slowly came to realise that I preferred my own company to the stress of trying to fit in and gain the approval of others. It took me until I got to uni to finally feel that way, though. School and college were a write-off."

"And now?"

"Now?" she repeats.

"How do you feel now?"

"I'm still socially awkward, but I don't care." She manages a smile. "When I was with Jack, it didn't matter. The two of us together felt like a team. We were our own clique. Jack and I were so easy in each other's company. There was no need for anyone else for either of us. Or at least that's what I thought."

That statement invites further exploration.

"Did something happen to make you doubt that?"

"Uh, no. I shouldn't have said anything." She pauses. "I was possessive sometimes, selfish, maybe. With him being away so often, I tended to let my thoughts run wild."

She smiles and waves her hands in a tiny gesture of exaggeration.

"Nothing changes, huh?" she half-jokes. "It would be funny if it weren't so tragic."

I can see her expression is reflecting on the sad truth rather than the comical fiction.

"Did you think Jack was seeing someone else?"

It's a direct question, and after Sophie's previous walk-out, I'm not sure it's the right one to ask. Still, some questions need to be asked, and some issues need to be brought out into the open.

160

"No," she says, quickly, and then, shaking her head, "Yes. Yes, I did."

Now we are getting somewhere, aren't we, Sophie? You've started to talk, but how much are you willing to say?

CHAPTER TWENTY

Jack.

I hadn't planned on telling Thacker anything about your little indiscretions, but somehow, he gets these things out of me. My sessions are about me, not you, but the more I talk about my issues, the more I seem to say about you.

Jane (I know you hate me calling her that, but you're not here and I can say what I like now) doesn't take up much of my thoughts now. She made a huge effort, after she came back from Arkhangelsk, to be friendly and kind and sympathetic. Imagine that, after everything that happened? She was the last person I wanted to see, but when she came over, she was so perfectly kind and gentle, I almost felt guilty for the resentment I've had towards her for such a long time. Almost.

When I first became suspicious of you and her, I gradually started to see signs that you were lying to me. All those evenings you worked late, all the times you were away when you couldn't connect to video chat with me. *No internet signal, sorry Sophie, no can do tonight.* All the times I pictured the two of you together. There's no way of knowing the truth now. Whatever the two of you did, I don't know when it started, and I can never be certain that it ended.

I know it has ended now. That's the only certainty I have.

Jane came round here, two days after she returned from the *tundra*, full of sympathy and platitudes. You know the type of thing. *If there's anything I can do for you, call me anytime.*

In the nights following, I sat in front of the muted television at three in the morning, watching silent loops of dismal programmes with the accompanying sign language. I watched the men and women sign their way through property shows, reality TV, whatever was on. It was them and me, night after night. Once I even thought about learning sign language myself, making it my new career. Of course, you know how my stupid ideas end up.

Anyway, one night I thought about testing her offer. *Anytime,* she said. *Anything.* Yes. Tell me all the details. Tell me exactly what happened between you and my husband. Tell me why he chose Arkhangelsk and you over home and me.

Tell me where he is now.

Do you know?

Do you know?

I can still picture the scene, as it would have run out. Me, sitting in my pyjamas, screaming down the phone, while she lay in her dark bed, somewhere across town, somewhere that you had probably, once, twice, many times, lay with her.

Do you know where he is, Jane?

Do you know?

It's never crossed my mind to question whether it is Jane that I see in every shadow, whether it could be her stalking me, watching every move I make. Do you want to know why, Jack? She has her own life.

Jane, whatever I think of her, is an independent, self-assured woman. I don't think she could care less about what I am doing. Why would she? She had what she wanted, and that had nothing to do with me. She didn't care about me when she was screwing you, and I can't begin to believe she would care about me now.

I flit from being certain I'm being watched to being certain it's all in my head. I don't know. Maybe I never will.

After you called it off with her, or at least after you told me that you did, you kept reassuring me that the two of you had to maintain a purely platonic and professional relationship. But even when the sex was extracted from your *relation-ship*, I still sometimes thought she spent more time with you than I did. It wasn't far from the truth. I wouldn't have wanted to be with you in the Arctic Circle, that's for sure, but if we could have been hanging out in New York or Spain? Well, that would be a different story.

I felt guilty, almost, for having a job that didn't allow me to book holidays on demand. Only being able to have my weeks off when the school was shut between terms was one of the definite down-sides of my job. I couldn't skip away and join you on any of your trips, not even as a hanger on, float-ing around your hotel room while you got on with the important work out in the field. All I could do was to stay at home, keep going to work, and com-ing home to an empty Jack-less house. And all the time, she was with you.

Of course, I was jealous.

It's easy to let your imagination run riot when your husband is in a hotel on another continent with another woman. You and I were supposed to be the team. You were the only one who ever made me feel part of something. Our relationship was everything to me, but you made me believe it was nothing to you.

I can't imagine I would ever have spoken these words to you out loud. I hid my feelings about Jane as much as I possibly could. My time with you was too important to pollute with negativity and nit-picking. When I told you I wanted you to stay at home with me instead of going to Arkhangelsk because I missed you too much to let you leave, that was true. It wasn't simply that I didn't want you to be there with her; it was that I wanted you to be here with me.

You had your dreams, and I had mine. I only wish we had them together.

Whatever happened or didn't happen, I'm the one that has ended up being sorry. I am here alone, and you are gone. She can't have you, but neither can I. That's not something I'm ready to talk to my psychiatrist about just yet.

I miss you always.

Soph

CHAPTER TWENTY-ONE

The word fidelity comes from the Latin *'fides'*, meaning *'faith'*. We expect our chosen partner to be faithful to us, and we have faith in them that they will. Fides was actually the name of the goddess of trust and good faith in Roman paganism. Then again, it doesn't take an etymologist to work out that Serena comes from the same root as *'serene'*, and my dear ex-lover was really anything but. Skip the faithful, skip the serene.

These are the things you don't know about someone when you first meet them. When we present ourselves to a new acquaintance, particularly when we want them to think favourably about us, we accentuate the positives, and suppress the negatives. At least I used to, back when I cared. Now, I'm brutally honest with everyone I meet, and look, I am alone.

Some time after the start of gym sessions, and before the day she walked out, the serenity began to fade. She picked up with a group of girls she'd known at college and started going out with them at weekends. Weekend nights out spread into weeknight wine and movies. Eventually, she was barely home. That's not what got me, though. What really did it for me was that she stopped caring. Her absence stung, but the practicalities of our life were slipping. The washing wasn't getting done. There was no one to cook, so I muddled along. When she was home, she would still leave it to me. After eating, she took herself off to the sofa to watch some trashy television programme or sit reading a throwaway supermarket shelf thriller.

"What's going on?"

I left it until ten minutes before bedtime on a Sunday evening to ask. Not great timing, but after a weekend of her being out, and me being at home, alone with my thoughts, I couldn't hold back any longer.

At first, she just gave me that look. You know, the *don't-start-not-now* look women have as soon as you want to have a serious conversation. And it *was* serious. I couldn't bear it any longer. It was time to confront her.

I knew what was going on. Not just the suspicion, but by the time I confronted her, I had gathered the proof.

"Don't," she said, as though she could cut off the conversation just like that.

Her book was still in her hand, and I couldn't bear it. I walked over to her, not quite storming over because she was only a couple of paces away from where I was sitting. With one upward flick of my hand, I launched the book into the air, and it flew across the room, landing by the door.

"What the hell?" Her face was flush with indignation. I hadn't planned on flipping the book, it was an instinctive move.

It was better than hitting her.

"This is important." I tried to keep my voice as even as possible, because all I wanted to do was yell at her. Standing over her, though, I couldn't help letting my antagonism boil to the surface. I crouched, bringing myself to eye level with her, and moved my face up close to hers.

"Tell me what's going on," I repeated.

I could feel her shallow, rapid breaths against my face. She pulled back, trying to move away from me, but there was nowhere for her to go. The armchair wouldn't allow her any space, and I wasn't going to move.

"Get off," she said, even though I wasn't touching her. "Get up. Get away."

"Stop avoiding the question, Serena," I said. "I want to know what's happening, and you're not leaving this room until you tell me."

Taking the direct line didn't seem to be working. Despite the fact I had her cornered, she wasn't talking.

172

"Who is he?"

"What? Get away. Go on. Stop this."

She pushed her hands into my chest and sent me toppling backwards onto the floor.

"You..." I was going to shout; I was going to swear. Instead, I forced myself not to. I wasn't going to let her get the better of me. "That wasn't nice, Serena. It wasn't necessary."

"Then don't be so stupid," she said.

"Stupid," I said, keeping my voice calm and controlled. "You're screwing around and I'm the one who's stupid?"

She must have already known that I knew what was going on. I guessed that by the way she avoided the question, but still, when I confronted her with it, she managed to laugh.

"Is that what this is about?"

As if she didn't know.

"What do you want me to say? I've thought about this moment, you know. I've thought about what I was going to say to you when you found

173

out, and you know what, I decided to just admit to it. There's no point trying to hide it, is there? You know I'm not happy in this relationship. You're not happy either. What it comes down to, though, is that you don't have the balls to do anything about it. And I do."

I was still on my backside on the floor, looking up at her as though I were some kind of prey she had brought down and was crouched over. I wished I were still in the dominant position, because then at least I would have something. I wouldn't be the silly little man on the ground with nothing left, not even his pride.

"Why didn't you leave me then? Why carry on with this? Why go behind my back and…?" I was desperately flailing for words. "… disrespect me like this?" I knew how I sounded, and it was unbearable. I coughed, clearing my throat, and channelled my most assertive self. "I don't want to know the details. I want you to leave."

I didn't. I didn't want her to go, but I didn't want her to have been cheating on me. Once the truth was out, there was no way back.

You can't always get what you want.

"Is that it? Is that all you have to say? You're pathetic." She spat the words at me as I was pulling myself up to my feet. Despite everything she had done, it was, apparently, I who was in the wrong.

There were so many words I could say, but none of them seemed like they would make any difference. There was nothing left to save, and I didn't want to save it, anyway. Not then. As soon as I knew what she had done, she was like a different person to me. By the end of the week, she had moved out of the flat. No paperwork to go through, no assets to split, no children to fight over. One day we were living together, and the next, she was gone.

My life was shattered, but I had to carry on. I had work to focus on. I got to keep the flat, after buying out her share. There were lots of positives, despite the pain.

Some men might build walls and put up barriers to future relationships, but not me. I've only ever wanted to find the One and make her happy. Although it sounds terrible, in a way I'm glad Sophie has been through it too. We have a shared experience; I know it's going to bring us closer. She will understand the way I feel about fidelity because Jack let her down too.

Next time around, it's going to be better for both of it. I'll make sure of it.

CHAPTER TWENTY-TWO

Jack.

I wasn't sure I could do it, but today was my first day back at work. Can you believe Susie kept my job open for all this time? Even though I've barely been able to bring myself to reply to her emails or pick up the phone when she calls, she was as nice as pie when I got in touch with her. There must be so many people better qualified than I am: more experienced, and certainly more well-balanced. Deep down, I guess she must like me after all.

I phoned her on Tuesday, and she said I could go in the following Monday. Pretty bad timing because it's the week before the holidays, but at least it means I'm back.

Back! Can you believe it?

When Thacker suggested it, the idea of returning seemed impossible. Starting the week before

Summer seemed pointless, until I realised that if I didn't do it then, I was going to have to wait almost two months to dive back in.

I had let myself get used to sitting around at home, thinking about what happened, wishing you were here. I couldn't begin to imagine what it would be like going back to school, being around other people all day. I've become so used to being alone, I barely know how to interact with other humans anymore. Having to stand in front of class after class of excitable, inquisitive kids felt like too much to get my head around. I expected the worst, of course, because that's just how my mind works.

It wasn't nearly as bad as I expected.

Nothing has changed at Broadoak. Nothing much, anyway. Fiona is on maternity leave now. I don't think you even knew she was pregnant. A lot can happen in a few months. Maybe that's why Susie was so keen to have me back. Another woman down, more work for the rest of them. I'm being harsh; Susie has been wonderful.

I didn't really *want* to go back. Still, returning makes me feel like I'm moving on, even though I'm going backwards, stepping into the shoes of last year's Sophie, the Sophie that lived here with her husband. I'm the Sophie that lives alone now. I'm the Sophie without a husband, the Sophie who sees a psychiatrist.

Last night, I spent far too long thinking about what it would be like facing up to my colleagues for the first time. Today though, I didn't even have the chance to worry about stepping foot in the staff room. Susie pulled me into her office as soon as I walked through the main door.

"Sophie, darling!" You know what she's like, such an over-the-top gushy love. "Here, here, here."

She ushered me through to her room. Still the same as it's always been.

"Shall we have a coffee and chat before you start to settle back into things?" she said.

I'd stopped for a Coffee Express on the way. That was my old routine, wasn't it? One of the things I liked best about working at Broadoak was being able to duck in for a latte on my walking commute. That doesn't say a lot about the job, but you know that I've always been a work-to-live rather than live-to-work kind of person. Not like you. I can't imagine there are many Coffee Express franchises in the Arctic Circle. They're probably missing a trick there. What could be better than a venti hot chocolate after a day on the tundra? This is where you would laugh at me and tell me, *"You're hysterical, Soph."* I'm sure when you were posted in New York you grabbed as many lattes as any other normal human.

Anyway, I'm veering off the point here. I agreed to her offer, and I sat, feeling awkward and out of place in the Headteacher's office. Even though I was there as a member of staff, I still felt the echo-memories of all the kids pulled in there for the serious talks and dispensations of detentions. It was nothing like that, though. Susie was gentle and friendly, and the coffee was good.

"I've had a word with them," Susie told me. She didn't need to be a mind-reader, I'm sure it was obvious I would be concerned about what my colleagues would think about me. "No one is going to ask any awkward questions."

For a moment, I considered leaping to the defence of my co-workers. As if any of them would make my return difficult. Then I remembered how office culture could skirt around the edges of toxicity. When Sandra and her husband got divorced, sure we all wanted to be supportive and caring and all that, but we also wanted to gossip. When we share communal break areas and have nothing more meaningful discuss, isn't it natural for us to talk about other people's lives? I know I've probably been a great source of gossip and speculation over the past few months. I hope they have enjoyed speculating on your location, and on how my mental health is holding up.

I nodded and said a quiet thank you.

"Any trouble, you come straight to me, okay?"

I felt like I was on my first day back after a prison sentence, not an extended break due to...

losing you

depression

an ongoing mental health crisis

...everything that's been going on.

"Okay." I wanted to start back out on a confident, positive vibe, but Susie somehow managed to crush that out of me just by being supportive. I know she means well, she always does, but maybe it would have been better to throw me into the ocean and see if I could remember how to swim. If I let the sharks bite me, that would have been down to me.

I was about to stand up and brace for my entrance to the staff room when she stopped me.

"One more thing," she said.

"Yes?" I could hear my voice tremble as I spoke, and I hated sounding so weak. "Yes?" I repeated, more confidently.

"That's the spirit," she smiled. "Look, I left everything on your desk exactly as it was when you were last here."

My little room, tucked away in what used to be a storage cupboard, blinged up with a kettle and a large jar of instant coffee. I nodded, wondering where she was going with this.

"Sandra suggested there were some things I might want to move, or tidy away for you." She looked me dead in the eye, and I held the gaze as she continued. "I told her it was up to you to decide whether to change things, I mean whether you want to…" It was her turn to be flustered, so I threw her a lifeline.

"The photos of Jack?" I said, without missing a beat.

"Yes," she hovered. "I hope I did the right thing."

I gave her a wide smile and nodded. "You did. Thank you."

And then I was ready. Off to the staff room and then onwards towards my first day back.

You would be proud of me, I know. You always celebrated even the tiniest of my victories. I should have been happy for you too, I realise that now, but I couldn't bear the thought of losing you again. I couldn't let you leave me. I had to find a way to stop you. I just couldn't see how.

I'm trying to heal. I'm moving on, but I'm not leaving you behind.

What's done is done, but Jack, I miss you. I miss us.

I'm sorry.

Sophie

CHAPTER TWENTY-THREE

I'm intrigued to hear whether going back to work has been a change for the better or the worse for Sophie. She'll either come in full of confidence and chatter, or she will have been drained and demoralised by the experience. It was a risk, suggesting she go, but encouraging her to get her life back on track could be exactly what she needs.

I'm about to find out.

"So how was it? You went back yesterday?"

She nods.

"Part time?"

"Three days a week. Uh-huh."

"I think that's an amazing start, Sophie.

"It was a lot easier than I expected." She smiles. There's an edge to her today; a positive change. "I didn't even think they would let me go back at such short notice. I don't think they would have if they weren't desperate." Now, she even

185

manages a laugh. "It's good to be out of the house."

"Would you like to tell me about it?"

Sophie shrugs. "There's not a lot to tell, really. I was nervous in the morning, of course, before I went out. Actually, I was more worried about what people were going to say, though. You know, what the other teachers, and especially the kids, might think of me. They all know what happened, well, at least the bits I'd told the Head, but you know what gossip is like."

I've never believed in the line *'there's only one thing worse than being talked about, and it's not being talked about'*. Having other people discuss your private life, or gossip about you behind your back is the worst.

"And what did they say?"

"Everyone was really nice. The kids that bothered to say anything told me it was good to have me back. One girl even came to my office door at break time to tell me, alone, that she had missed me. I almost cried after she had left. I can't believe I was away for so long."

"And the other teachers?"

"Well, like I say. I keep myself to myself mostly, so I didn't get into any deep conversations. It's all been friendly chatter and supportive words. The number of people that have told me to give them a shout if I need anything. They were never that nice to me before. I should have done this a long time ago."

"Gone back to work?"

"Uh, yes. Gone back to work."

"You seem positive. I have to ask, though. Did you have any of the feelings you have been experiencing while you were at work? That someone is watching?"

Sophie shakes her head resolutely.

"Not once. Can you believe it?"

"That's excellent. Why do you think that might be?"

Immediately, her excitement and mood both drop.

"What?" she says.

"It's okay, Sophie. It's not a trick question. I'm not trying to trip you up or bring you down. I'm interested in your opinion. Why do you think you didn't have any of those feelings?"

"You think whoever is watching me can't get to me in the school? Is that..." She looks visibly shocked, and I'm worried for a moment she's about to slam into a panic attack. The colour drains from her face.

"Sophie. It's okay. Try to stay calm. You went back to work. You felt supported by your colleagues and the kids. You didn't experience any of the delusions you have been having over the past few months. I wanted to hear whether you think there could be a link there."

"Okay, okay," she repeats, trying to talk herself down. "I just... I thought you were... I suppose I'm still pretty sensitive." She's not managing to

188

smile yet, but she fans her face with her hand and appears to settle a little.

There's a long pause, and eventually she speaks.

"Maybe." The word falls tentatively.

"Was it on your mind when you were going to work?"

She nods. "I barely slept the night before. I thought..." She thinks, and then continues. "I didn't want to leave the house. I was worried about... Uh, I didn't know how I was going to get through the day. But I told myself, do it for Jack. Get out there and do it for him. When I was on my way there, I was doing my usual looking over my shoulder, imagining ghosts in the shadows." She says it as though it bores her. "When I got to school, there was so much to think about, so much to do, that I forgot about home."

"You forgot about being watched?"

Home. She said home.

"Yes, that's what I meant. Look at the state of me. I really thought I was getting it together."

"You are. This is such good progress, Sophie. You're doing so well."

She's shaking her head in a way that shows she doesn't believe the words.

"I'm not. I never do well. Not at anything. I'm never good enough. Ugh, listen to me. This is what I'm like. I whine and complain and..."

"Sophie, please..."

"No. It's obvious why Jack left, isn't it? The police were right. He had enough of me, took off and disappeared rather than going through the drawn-out trauma of divorce. Because I wouldn't have made it easy."

"You had discussed divorce?"

This is a revelation. I wonder why she hasn't mentioned it earlier. A man disappearing when he's about to split from his wife sounds far less suspicious than a happy husband randomly vanishing.

"I saw it getting closer, and I tried to hang onto him. Even after everything, I still wanted to be with him. I didn't want to let go." She is teetering on the brink of tears again and pauses to reach over for a tissue from the box on the desk. A good psychiatrist is always prepared.

"I found out all about the two of them. Him and Jane. She was someone from work, what a cliché. It was over, before he vanished. Or at least he said it was. Even though he wasn't with Jane anymore, when it happened... well, you know... being alone must be better than being with me."

"And do you feel this woman, Jane, is to blame for this?"

"No. We were drifting apart before he met her. And it wasn't entirely his fault either."

"So, let me check with you that I'm interpreting this as you mean it. You feel like you were partly to blame for his infidelity?"

Sophie breaks eye contact, and I can tell she's trying to hold back her tears. I can see the wet trickle around the corner of her eyes.

"It sounds stupid when you say it like that. But he was away so often and when he was home, he spent less and less time with me. We had a kind of home office out in the garden, he kept all his equipment out there. When he had to work from home, there was too much of his stuff flooding the house, so we thought it was a worthwhile invest-ment. It even has its own bathroom. He didn't even need to come back into the house to... well, you get the idea. Some weekends I only saw him at mealtimes and bedtime." She shakes her head. "I don't know how I let it happen."

There are still ten minutes left on the clock, and it's never good to let a session end on a negative note. With seven full days to fill until the next meeting, that's too long to let someone dwell on what they've said, on thoughts they've had, and on what they have done.

Time to change direction.

"Why don't we move on to something that might not be so difficult for you to talk about?"

I can tell by the look on her face that she's not convinced by this line. Still, it's worth a try.

"How about you tell me about when you first met? Tell me how you got together."

"Oh," she says, shuffling slightly in her chair, repositioning her body, letting her physical stance reflect this change in direction. "Right. Okay. I could do that."

"No pressure. Start wherever you feel most comfortable and let's see where it goes."

I know this apparent easy-in is a gateway to so much more. It sounds like an easy question, but it's a way of gathering background information that might shed light on what's happened and what's happening now.

"I'm not sure it's a particularly interesting story."

"I don't know. A teacher and a geologist? Not an obvious match. How did it all begin?"

"He was with a couple of friends. One of them was Jane, who I assumed was his girlfriend. How ironic is that? He assured me that they were work colleagues, nothing romantic going on, but in the early days of our relationship, he always laughed about my assumption. I didn't think it was a weird conclusion to jump to really, and looking back, of course I was totally justified. I don't want any bonus points for predicting my husband's infidelity though. After I got to know Jane, I never believed that Jack would be interested in her. I didn't believe it until it happened."

Nod. Don't say anything. Don't break the flow.

"Anyway. When we first met, I didn't want to let him go. I went from knowing nothing about him to wanting to know everything. His life seemed so interesting, you know. I mean, not the rocks and stuff. The actual detail of what he did. Travelling the world. I guess that was it. I haven't been any further than the county border. I was born here, went to school here, did my B.Ed. at the University just outside of town. I've never lived anywhere outside a twenty-mile radius from where I was born. Jack travelled the world."

"And that was what drew you to him?"

"Not necessarily, no. But it certainly made him more interesting than most of the men I run into."

She's talking about him in the past tense, I notice, but nobody is bringing that up. Not right now.

Time is coming to an end. Sophie knows it because she glances up towards the clock.

It's probably best to end before she starts talking about Jane again. Try to end on a positive.

"That was a tough one, today," she says, letting out a sigh.

"Well done, Sophie. It must have been difficult for you to go back to work, and difficult to open up here today."

She nods and stretches to a slight smile.

Session over. Another one in the bag. She's starting to open up, and her confidence is growing all the time.

She scoops up her jacket and heads out of the door.

When she leaves, I can't control my emotion any longer. I get up, give the chair – the closest thing to me – a firm, hard kick and send it flying across the room.

If there weren't people in the next room that could hear, I would yell – but there are people in there and I'm in control.

It's all very well turning up and giving the chat, but she's still intent on hiding the truth. The more she says, the more aware I am of what she isn't saying. If she doesn't dig deeper, I'm going to have to force her. It's time she stopped hiding and started talking about what really happened.

CHAPTER TWENTY-FOUR

Jack.

I thought I was safe at work. That feeling I get when I leave the house had stopped, earlier in the week when I got to the school. But today, I could feel him watching. And yes, of course it's not you. How could it be? I don't know what I was thinking. I'm going to stick with *he* from now on, because I know it must be a man. Don't ask me how, but I'm sure of this. Remember all those little hunches I used to have, those gut feelings that always turned out to be right?

Last day of term, I finished work late. Typical me. One of the girls from year eleven was meant to be getting a lift home with her friend and something happened between them last lesson. I didn't bother to ask what it was, and don't judge me, but I didn't actually care. She turned up at my office at half-past three, just as I was about to pick up my bag and head out of the door. Well, I could hardly leave her there, could I? It's not like I have a husband waiting for me to get home to make his dinner now; all I have are microwave meals and Netflix.

This girl's mum was on a business trip somewhere and her dad lives on the other side of town. Bit of a move up in the world, into those new apartments opposite the church. Maybe we would have moved there too if things hadn't turned out the way they have. I called him up and I swear he was about to tell her to find her own way home. I don't think he realised he was on speakerphone, and I could hear every word he said to her. Out of sight and out of mind and all that. He's probably got a very busy and important life that doesn't involve his daughter anymore.

"Sorry to inconvenience you," I said, when he came to collect her, even though the inconvenience was most certainly mine.

He didn't even thank me for waiting around with her. Ungrateful idiot.

So, I was in a stormy mood already when I locked up and made my way off school grounds and onto Belle Vue Avenue. I always try to stay on the wide roads now, nowhere with bushes along the edges, no narrow passageways where people could loiter.

Even still, when I got down to the crossroads, where Belle Vue meets Acacia, I realised there was no one else around. Or, more to the point, there was someone around. The streets were quiet in both directions, a couple of cars, but no one on the pavements except me. I could *feel* him, though. It's like a tickle at the back of my neck, almost as though his stare is stroking me, teasing me.

There's that layby on Acacia, outside the entrance to the children's playground there, the one where you can get those ice cream wafers if you get there early enough on the weekends. Anyway, from the crossroads, that part of the pavement, where it curves in towards the park, is hidden from view. I'm sure that's where he was standing. I think if he positioned himself exactly right, he would be able to watch me walking down there, waiting at the crossing, and making my way across the road without me ever seeing him. But I knew, I just knew.

I tried to play it cool, act like I didn't see him there, like everything was fine, but I could feel my heart pounding and I was sure my legs were going to buckle. I pressed the button on the pedestrian crossing and stared at the red man symbol, urging it to switch to green. I was trying my best to keep looking forwards, not to give him the satisfaction of looking up the street in his direction, but I couldn't stop myself. I had to look. I had to find out for sure I wasn't imagining it.

Psychosis!

Just think about Doctor Thacker's reaction when I can tell him that actually I don't need his help anymore, thank you very much.

See, I'm not imagining it, I actually have my very own stalker.

I looked. For a split second, without even turning my head, I let my eyes dart up Acacia and scan the shadows by the side of the street. This time, I almost saw him. I caught the slightest hint of movement, just a dark flicker before the crossing started to beep, and I snapped my eyes forwards, quickened my pace, and carried on home as fast as I could manage.

I needed you there when I got back to our house. I wanted to fall into your arms, let you hug me as I buried my head and cried against your chest.

"He was there," I would tell you. "He was there."

And you would hold me, stroke my hair and whisper, "I know, I know."

But I didn't see anyone for certain. There's no proof. There are no photographs. I'm in exactly the same position that I was before.

If you were here, you would tell me to calm down, to not be so melodramatic, to think rationally about all of this. That's your forte though, isn't it? Rational thought. You followed science around the world, leaving me here, always, with my stupid anxious brain and crazy ideas.

Anxious, yes. Crazy? I don't know. I hope not.

If you were here, I wouldn't be afraid. I wouldn't turn all the lights on when I get into the house, checking in each room, looking into cupboards, behind the shower curtain, once I even opened the hatch to the loft. I pulled down the ladder - remember how much I hate climbing up there - and made myself pop my head into the dusty space. I was coughing for half an hour afterwards. You would have laughed, I know, and I would have pretended to be cross with you until we both ended up in fits of laughter. I've forgotten what laughter feels like. It's been so long. There's been so little to feel happy about since you've been gone.

Nothing has changed. I still don't know what is happening to me. I still want to believe you're coming home. I want to believe that one day I'll get a phone call, or I'll hear your key turning in the lock. I'd run to the door so quickly that I'd end up slamming into you in my usual clumsy way. I wouldn't care. Not one bit.

Delusions. More delusions.

S.

CHAPTER TWENTY-FIVE

I know the saying is that we always hurt the ones we love, but I always seem to be on the receiving end of the pain. The ones I love are the ones that hurt me the most.

I'm a grown man, in my thirties. I'm not going to pretend there have been many women in my life though. There were only a couple of brief flings through college and university, and then a desert-like dry spell until I met Serena. I wasn't looking for a relationship. Living in a decent flat, working in a decent job and watching classic thriller movies until it was time to go to bed, sleep, wake, rinse repeat: it was enough.

Those other women hurt me, for sure, but so much time has passed that I don't dwell on those experiences now. Serena, on the other hand, is a recent wound. I've dealt with her by fixating on Sophie. I accept that. I admit that.

Going home alone at the end of the day, I humour myself by shouting "Hey, Sophie," as I enter the hallway. "I'm home." We won't call each other honey or have silly pet names. Not like some couples do. Anyway, that's for the future. Now, she never hears me. She doesn't hear me during her sessions, and she doesn't hear me shouting out to her in my empty home.

Why her? Why Sophie? I could have hung my infatuation onto any number of women. In another life, perhaps it would have been Lola or Henny. But in this life, it couldn't be anyone other than Sophie. Right place, right time, right woman.

Her words from today's session are still fresh in my mind as I step into the bathroom and strip off. It's something I always do as soon as I get home. All that time, working in a dirty, contaminated environment, I need to get it off me as quickly as I can. Just because I'm interested in Sophie's life doesn't mean I don't take time to reflect on my own. I know I have issues, but we all do.

It's just a question of how deeply they run in the vein and whether we let anyone dig them out or not.

Sophie has an almost impenetrable exterior. The thrill of the chase and the challenge of cracking her open must factor in my obsession with her, on some level, but I'd rather leave her deceptive side buried.

Suddenly, I jump, and almost slip backwards in the shower. My lack of concentration has let me turn the water temperature up too high, and the scorching pulse is searing my skin. I try to hold back a swear word - I know she can't hear me, but I always try to be the sort of person that could deserve her – and ram my hand hard against the temp control.

This is what you do to me.

I wanted her to work through everything at her own pace, I really did, but not only is she dragging her heels through every session, she's also decided to lie, lie, lie.

206

No good can come of it.

It doesn't change the way I feel about her, but she needs to accept what she's done. If she can't face up to what happened to Jack, and finally tell the truth, I think she actually might lose her mind after all.

CHAPTER TWENTY-SIX

Jack.

This is going to come as a bolt from the blue, I know, but I finally caved in and messaged Jane. She told me to call anytime, and finally the time seemed right.

I can almost hear you gasp in amazement. You know how things were between me and her. I don't forgive and forget, especially when it comes to you. I know that you would probably expect me to never want to see her face, but I have to. I have to talk to her, properly this time, about you.

I thought it over for a long time before I found the courage. When she came round that time, just after she got back from Arkhangelsk, I wasn't ready to talk to her. All I could think about was the aching hole in my life without you here. Trying to discuss anything with her would have been useless. I hated her so much right then that it might as well have been her that had taken you from me. To make it worse, she was abjectly perfect. She said all the right words and did everything a friend would do.

She isn't my friend, and she isn't ever going to be. Still, I had to contact her, and I have to see her.

I sat with the phone in my hand for a good twenty minutes, trying to work out what to say, wondering whether she would even reply. I know when she gave me her number, it was one of those polite gestures that no one ever expects anyone to call them up on. The same as *'pop in if you're ever in town'*. I have to be honest, though, her discomfort was never a factor.

It was easier once I'd slugged a hefty shot of vodka. You know I hate the stuff, but it was all you had left in the cupboard, and vodka seemed ironically fitting, given the circumstances. A good old Russian drink.

I tapped the words "I'm sorry" into my phone and then sat and stared at them. Was I apologising for the way I treated her, or for what I did to you? I made up my mind the first time we met that I wasn't going to like her. All I could see was the way the two of you looked at each other, laughed together at your stupid little inside jokes, made me feel just like I had all that time in school, college, university. You were meant to be different. You were meant to make me *feel* different. But when it came down to it, you were just the same as everyone else.

There's nothing between us.

You told me that so many times. Perhaps it was never true.

It took her a full day to reply to me. At first, I thought she was going to ignore it. After ten minutes had passed, and then an hour, I was certain I had made a mistake. What was I doing messaging her in the first place? I felt like an idiot. I went to bed, got up the next day, and there was still no response. Shrug it off, I thought, and told myself I had tried. At least I had tried. I went about my day: from home to work, from work to home, and the usual evening in front of the television alone. As time went on, thoughts of Jane and my foolish attempt at communication slipped from my mind. So much so I actually jumped in my chair when my phone beeped with the sound of an incoming text.

Barely anyone sends me messages now. Not that I was ever the social butterfly, but once the initial flurry of attention settled, after you disappeared, my phone fell silent, almost as if it were in mourning for the loss of you.

You want to know what her message said? I know you do.

"You have nothing to be sorry for."

I thought I would feel better, clearing the air, but all I got was this sinking dissatisfaction. I don't know what I expected, but her response was anticlimactic. I wanted more from her. I deserve more.

But, on the other hand, I think she was right. I do have nothing to be sorry for. It was the two of you that caused this whole situation. If you hadn't got caught up in your infatuation, perhaps you would have stayed faithful to me. What did Plain Jane ever have that I didn't? That's the question I'm meant to ask, isn't it?

She and I are two very different people. I know that, and part of me believes you only wanted her because she wasn't me, because she was an exotic *other*.

Because she was someone else's.

The two of you started something neither of you should have ever entered into. And now it feels as though she is all I have left of you. She's my only connection. The little pieces you left with her that you should have left with me. The traces of you that are still tangled around her. The memories you created with her, when your whole life should have been about me, me, me.

That's why I want to talk to her. I want *her* memories too. I want to suck her dry of you. I want to work out what happened, what went wrong, what I did wrong.

I've come to the realisation though, that I want her to know what I've done. I can't see any other way out of it. My plan never had an end point.

If I tell her, something has to happen. I have no idea what that something is, but it will be a way out of this mess, one way or another.

I'm going to have to tell her the truth.

Wish me luck, Jack.

S.

CHAPTER TWENTY-SEVEN

I'm not in the mood for Thursday, but it comes around anyway, as Thursdays tend to do. Time is more reliable than people are. It slowly plods forwards, carrying us with it towards our fates. Whether we change those fates through our actions, for better or for worse, is down to us.

This is the random melancholia I'm stuck in today. Even though I'm distracted and distant, Lola still tries to make conversation. Perhaps it's *because* I'm distracted and distant that she tries so hard.

"Everything alright, sir?" she asks.

I'm hovering near the reception desk. My brain can't quite seem to remember where I am supposed to be going, or what I was meant to be doing.

"Sir?" She looks at me, and then calls Henny, dragging her attention away from her crossword book. "Bev. Beverley." That's Henny's real name, though I never use it. Calling her *Beverley* makes her sound like someone's elderly aunt. No one is called Beverley nowadays.

"What's..." Before she can finish the sentence, she sees me swaying, and darts around the edge of the desk to meet me.

"Sir," she says, addressing me as she and Lola always do, but with a more anxious tone than I've heard before. "Sir, sit down. You don't look well."

"Really, I'm fine," I say, but maybe I'm not.

Lola lowers me gently into a chair, her chair as it happens, and through my confused fog, I see her gesturing towards Henny.

I don't know how long I sit, propped against the reception desk, but it's not long enough for either of the women to seek out proper medical attention for me. Not that I needed it, but if I had, I think I would have been screwed. Their professional development plans need to be updated with what to do in case of life-threatening emergencies. I could probably stick a few other items on their study plans too.

"He's coming round," Lola says to Hen, squawking into my ear.

"Are you alright? Can you hear me?" Henny waves her podgy hand in front of my face. Her wedding ring was clearly bought when she was a few sizes smaller, as the flesh oozes around it on either side. Focusing on this, however, slows my answer and causes Lola to chime in.

"Sir. Can you hear us?" The question from her comes loudly and slowly, as though she is trying to explain something to a foreign tourist.

"Yes, yes," I say, and my voice is tense and snappy in a way I hadn't intended. I concentrate on toning it down, and say, "Sorry. Thank you. Yes, I'm fine."

"Would you rather go home? Can I call you a taxi?"

Of course, they want to get rid of me. My paranoid mind skips to that conclusion before I focus again, forcing myself into a rational mindset.

"No," I say. "Really, I'm fine." Thinking quickly, I make up the first excuse I can concoct. "I missed breakfast," I tell them, and they look at each other, nodding. They really can be unknowingly comical. "I'll be fine."

"If you're sure?" Lola says.

In all honesty, I'm not sure. I had my usual breakfast: oats with honey and chopped nuts, a mug of coffee, and then a slice of wholemeal toast. Serena got me into that little combination, and even after she left, I kept the same routine. It works for me: quick and easy. All I can think of is that this is Sophie's fault. I wouldn't be feeling this way if it wasn't for her.

"Yes," I say. "Let's get on with it. Don't want to keep everyone waiting."

She and Henny exchange another look, as though trying to make a decision between themselves without verbal discussion. Whatever unspoken choice was made, Henny nods.

"Alright, Sir. If you need anything, you just let us know."

"Fine. Yes." All I feel now is embarrassment. I want to get away from them and into the office before anything else happens. I'm lucky there's no one else here yet. Imagine doing something this stupid in front of a packed waiting room.

"Thank you," I add, as I get up and push past them to the right side of the reception desk.

I make it into the office and try to get myself in the right frame of mind for the session. No tea today, a glass of water will do. Think calming thoughts and focus on the present moment. I'm not sure what happened to me, but I've got to focus. Look forwards and get through this appointment.

For the first time, I'm glad it's Jonah's session, not Sophie's. I'm not in any state to see her. I know something, though. This has gone on long enough. It's time for some truths to start coming out.

We begin with the standard openers, check-ins, and the monotonous details of Jonah's life. Jonah has completed his food diary like a good boy. Binge eating is the least of his problems, but at least it's one that can be quantified, measured and chipped away at. Everything else? Well, that's going to take a lot of sessions, and a lot of money, to resolve.

We skirt around the issues for the best part of the session. I sometimes feel as though the sessions are just an opportunity for him to have some social interaction, like he has so little else in his life he only comes to the office to make human contact. I've heard the way he talks to Henny and Lola, and I've heard what they say about him when he's out of earshot.

219

Men like him seem oblivious to how they appear to other people. He comes in, sits in his chair, and goes through the motions, never really achieving anything. Why do I keep seeing him? Well, I should hope the answer is obvious. Human motivation is a double-edged sword. Some humans are complicated and patently unknowable. Others are so transparent it's hard not to see right through them.

I've let myself get lost in my own thoughts, and I'm afraid I haven't been concentrating fully on our conversation. That's about to change dramatically, and the change begins like this.

"Everything we say in these sessions is confidential, isn't it?"

There's a pre-scripted answer to this question. Everything is confidential unless there's a need for disclosure. If someone tells their psychiatrist they are going to harm themselves, or harm another person, that whole right to confidentiality goes out of the window. Any professional has a duty to protect individuals and society.

"Do you plan to do any harm?" As a follow-up question, it's blunt and bang on the nose.

"No. It's not like that. I have something to tell you."

"Okay then, Jonah. Go ahead."

"You have to keep it to yourself. And it's going to be difficult for you."

"As long as you aren't putting yourself or anyone else at risk, your secret is safe with me. It won't be difficult, I promise."

But it will. It will.

The next sentence is the beginning of the end.

"Jack never went to Arkhangelsk."

CHAPTER TWENTY-EIGHT

It takes a few moments for the words to sink in.

"What did you say?"

"I know you heard me."

Heard, but didn't understand. The confusion of having one patient talk about a different person's life. Aren't they all supposed to stay in their own compartments? Separate, safe, isolated; not getting tangled up in other people's lives.

"Jack?"

"Jack. Jack Portman. Jack Richard Portman, if you're still confused. Not that you necessarily know his middle name, I suppose. It's ridiculous anyway, isn't it?"

"But…"

"He didn't go to Arkhangelsk. He didn't go missing in Arkhangelsk because he was never there."

"But…"

"The thing is, you just believe everything your patients say to you.

"How do you…? What do you know about Jack? And Sophie? You know Sophie."

The last sentence is a statement, rather than a question. It can't be coincidence that two patients know each other, surely.

"I think that's plenty for one day. I just wanted you to know."

So much confusion. So much to unravel.

Is there a risk of harm? And if so, who is at risk?

It's going to take some time for the words to settle. Jonah Washington and Sophie Portman are an unlikely pairing.

Jonah has to leave. He's said more than enough. He's out of the office, hurrying through reception, past Henny and Lola, and out onto the street.

"Beverley! Stop him."

Too slow.

Henny could drag herself up, waddle around the desk and give chase, but it's too late. Jonah is on his way and unavailable for further questions. It's time to start adding up the facts and working out what the hell is happening.

The first logical step is to check the records. There's no evidence of a Jonah Washington at the address on file. In fact, there's no sign of a Jonah Washington living in this town. False name, false address? Both? Would it even be a surprise if his mental condition is fictitious?

It doesn't say much about a psychiatric doctor that he can't pick up on when he is being blatantly lied to. Jonah has serious issues, but not necessarily the ones he admitted to. Where would you even start to piece this together?

Sophie and Jonah both booked in for their first visits in June. Two new patients within a week of each other. It's not uncommon: slots open up, referrals come in, patients make private appointments all the time. There wouldn't be any reason to suspect a connection between them. On the surface, all they have in common is that they prefer a morning visit. Could be coincidence. Probably is.

Sophie and Jonah are around the same age. Sophie is thirty-two, and, if you believe at least some of what Jonah filled in on his patient details form, he is thirty-three. So what? The average age of onset for mental health issues in mid-twenties, but it usually takes longer to seek help – or to be sent for it. Early thirties? Standard.

The elephant in the room – or not in the room – is Jack. The patient formerly known as Jonah knows Jack Portman, and it's patently evident he knows Sophie. Turn that around, work backwards, and there you have it. Sophie Portman knows Jonah.

"Bev. Call Sophie Portman. Ask her if she wouldn't mind coming in to see me, please."

"Do you want me to tell her why?"

Why not? Let her know that one of the other patients in the clinic seems to know more about her than they're supposed to. On the other hand, wouldn't it be better to see her reaction when she finds out? There's a lot to unpack, and perhaps it's better for everyone if that's done face-to-face.

"Uh, no. Tell her it's nothing to worry about."

As little white lies go, that's a fairly large, dark one.

I watch from outside the door, tucked out of sight, as they flap around the office like birds when hearing the crack of a shotgun. They'll be working on this for a while. I'm going to leave dear Doctor Thacker and his hapless assistants to try to put the pieces together. I've played the role of Jonah for long enough. Now, I need to be myself.

Sophie isn't going to make that appointment, unfortunately. I knew when I dropped the bombshell about Jack, that I would need to pay her a home visit. I've tried to stay away, not just for her, but for me too, but I know that I've been delaying the inevitable.

It's time for the truth.

CHAPTER TWENTY-NINE

I knew I would eventually have to go to Sophie's house, but I never thought it would be so soon. I'm banking on the fact Doctor Thacker is too impotent to leave his office and hotfoot it over there himself. He might be able to put two and two together, but working out the quadrilateral equation that connects me and Sophie, Jack and Serena is a different matter entirely.

I don't trust myself. I've imagined the scene in my head so many times, but actually walking down her neat little avenue, pushing open her gate and crossing the threshold onto her property is more daunting, and much more thrilling than I could have imagined.

It's a lovely home. Or at least from the outside, it appears that way. She's gone all out with the white-fenced cottage garden look, even though we are nestled in the suburbs of town. Looking more closely, the flower beds are speckled with the green bodies of sprouting weeds, and the roses are in desperate need of pruning. It's fine on the surface, but no one would have to look far to see the rot that's starting to set in. Always examining the details, obsessing over the little things; isn't that the root of my problems?

On a regular week, Sophie would be at work at this time, now she has returned, sleepwalking her way through the lessons, and then nestling down in her office room. I wanted to watch her there when she went back. It would have been perfect. My one-hour slot could have blossomed into a full working day, three times a week.

I quickly found out that it's too difficult to locate a chink in the armour of school security. I had a great plan. I thought I'd be able to stroll up to the reception hatch and sweet talk the frumpy assistant, just like I did with Henny and Lola.

"Oh, I have a daughter in Year Eleven," I said, leaning forward as far as I could into the gap in the wall. Getting close-up is one of my favourite techniques. I read that moving physically closer to someone can make them feel psychologically closer to you. At the school, though, it had the opposite effect. Now that I think about it, it's pretty dumb advice. It comes across as aggressive, not persuasive. That nugget of wisdom must have come from one of those *Influence Friends and Meet People* books I download free from the internet.

"Sir, can you step back?" the receptionist said.

I'm sure I saw her hand hover under the desk, where she undoubtedly had a panic button for when a harmless, charming man leaned too far into her precious little hatch. Or other such emergencies.

"Sorry," I said. Even though she was testing my patience, I kept smiling. I had to convince myself I had everything under control so that I didn't do anything stupid. A school is probably one of the worst places imaginable that I could Hulk out.

"That's alright. We have policies," she said, trying to smile back but failing.

I know the policies were an excuse to get me away from her, but whatever. I should have been more careful, and I knew it.

"What was the name of your daughter again, Mr..."

But it was already too late. Slipping into the school was difficult enough. The entrances and exits were all secure, and I could see there was no way the woman in the hatch was going to help me out. I don't give up easily as a rule, but being caught installing surveillance devices in a school is the kind of thing that can get a man into several years of trouble. It wasn't worth the risk.

I have been patient.

I watched Sophie in the psychiatrist's office as Doctor Thacker stumbled his way through session after session, wondering when he was ever going to get her to talk. Eventually though, my frustration got the better of me. It was like playing a guessing game, where you know you have to give someone a clue, even if it's against the rules. Thacker only saw me as Jonah Washington, irritating and obsessive. Psychiatrists are meant to listen to their patients, believe what they are telling them is the truth, and work with whatever they bring to the table. Six years or more of training and he still can't pick up on other people's lies. Not mine, and not Sophie's.

I may have dropped in a false name, but everything else I have said is true. Sophie, on the other hand, is a barefaced liar.

Not anymore. If we are going to have a future together, I want it to start with honesty. She's going to have to tell me what she did to Jack.

CHAPTER THIRTY

There's a neat little path running up the centre of the garden at the front of Sophie and Jack's house. It's an attractive property in a desirable area. The combined wages of a teacher and a research geologist must have worked out well for them. The red brick and white window frames are welcoming, and for a moment I almost believe I'm popping round to visit a friend. If things had happened differently, that would have been a reality. I could have strolled up to the front door, carrying a bottle of wine, looking forward to dinner, drinks, and intelligent conversation. Instead, I remind myself to look around, check whether any curtains are twitching, whether anyone has seen me arrive. I'm used to being the one who watches, and I know all too well that someone could be watching me.

It's such a momentous occasion for me, finally being here, that I have to stop to take it all in. Also,

I want to give my heart rate time to settle, like when you run up three flights of stairs to a meeting and then need to stand outside the room, getting back to that calm equilibrium before walking in.

I've thought about what I'm going to say to her. I've had such a long time to think about it that I've rehearsed this speech to the point of perfection. What I didn't account for is the feeling my heart is about to explode, the throbbing pounding in my chest that's forcing my temples to thud with pressure. I keep as steady as I can and keep walking.

With Jack being away so often, he and Sophie were clearly big on security, just like she told Thacker. The door is both heavy and heavily locked, and there's one of those video doorbells. I know where to stand to avoid the camera, so I position myself.

Waiting on her doorstep, I try to compose myself. I could use a paper bag to breathe into, to help me to slow myself down, get my body into an even tempo before I ring the bell. I can't show up red-faced and panting; seems like that's exactly what she would expect from a stalker.

I'm *not* a stalker. I haven't followed her around. When we almost met in the Kwik Shop, it wasn't my fault, and didn't I do everything I could to avoid her seeing me? I never wanted to cause her any distress. I've only ever wanted good things for her. When I said I have only seen her in the psychiatrist's office, it was the truth.

I press the buzzer.

I wait.

I wait some more.

There's no answer.

I can't believe Sophie would be anywhere else but here. This couldn't be the one time she actually has plans. I catch myself laughing at that little joke. Sophie never *has plans*. She has colleagues rather than friends, and she's so insecure and defensive that she shuts down, refuses to communicate, and turns any potential friend into an enemy.

Perhaps she's not that bad with everyone, but she definitely was with Serena. Okay, it turned out that she had just cause, but Sophie didn't know that, not back then.

By the time I press the buzzer for the second time, my excitement has already started to morph into frustration. She can hear the doorbell, so why isn't she answering? It's all very well to do this to a doorstep hawker, but when she does it to me, that's a different story altogether. I have to remind myself she doesn't know who's at the door, because I'm purposefully hiding from her line of video sight, and the thought calms me enough to ring again.

The buzzer sounds inside the house, a fake twinkling trill. I much prefer the classic doorbell, a solid confident ding-dong chime...

My thoughts are truncated, and I have to snap back into the moment as I hear footsteps inside, approaching the door. At last. I'm finally here, in front of her, on her own territory.

Sophie cracks the door open slightly.

She's in front of me.

I'm here.

"Hello?"

She isn't trying to conceal her annoyance at being disturbed. Her face is crumpled into a less than attractive sullen frown. I don't want to see that. I want to see her smile.

"Hello," I echo.

A smell of herbs and tomatoes oozes from the house. I must have come at an inconvenient time. She's probably got one of those crappy ready meals in the microwave. It's just gone ten in the morning; her schedule seems to have gone awry. Any second now I'll hear the ping of completion. Still, it can't be helped. I'm here now, and there's no time like the present.

"I'm sorry to interrupt your morning," I say. "But I think it's time the two of us had a talk."

She stares at me for a few seconds and doesn't speak. I'm starting to feel like a door-to-door salesman trying to persuade her to let me in so I can tell her all about how new windows could change her life.

"I'm making brunch," she says. And then, as if my last sentence has only just filtered into her brain, her expression shifts, and her frown looks more confused than annoyed. "Do I know you?"

I try to hold my smile. I try. I try, but that question hits me like a slap, and I can't do it. I can't.

"Sophie," I say, unable to mask the disappointment in my voice.

Whatever tells I gave off, I've spooked her. She takes a step backwards, away from the door, and reaches her hand out to push it closed. It's too late for that, though. As she moves back, I move forwards, almost as if the two of us are dancing there in the doorway. My foot blocks the door as she tries to shut me out.

"I'm sorry, Sophie," I say, and truly I am. "But you knew this was going to happen one day."

She's shaking her head as she tries again to push the door, realises the futility of the situation, and instead turns to run.

There's nowhere for her to go. The only other entrance is the back door, and I already know it will be securely locked. She's such a stickler for her safety that she has ended up being trapped by her own proficiency. I walk slowly through the door, taking my time to secure the locks, each one in turn, before I pace into the kitchen. As I thought, Sophie is fumbling the lock at the top of the back door.

"Don't do that, Sophie. There's really no point."

"Get away from me!" She kicks out, and I jump back from the circle of her reach.

"What's the point in trying to get away from this?"

I'm still trying to be calm. She's a scared animal right now, a deer in a clearing, trying to dart from the hunter. I shake my head at the thought.

239

That's not what I am. I'm a ranger. A helper. Her salvation, not her stalker.

"This what?" She has stopped trying to get her key into the door, although her hand is still holding onto it. "Who are you? What do you want?"

She's not looking at me; she's not trying to work the situation out. Instead, she turns her head, her eyes dart around the room, and I know she's looking for help. Something to defend herself with, perhaps, or a phone so she can call for help. She takes one last look out of the window, into the garden beyond, where her freedom lies just out of reach, before turning back to me.

I put my hands up in a calming gesture, as though I were walking towards that deer. Still, I step forward, causing her to move back against the door.

"It's okay, Sophie. I don't want to hurt you."

Don't want to probably doesn't sound as reassuring as I intended. It doesn't mean I *won't* hurt her, but really, that's not my plan right now. How could I ever think of harming Sophie?

"Who are you?" she asks again.

The question cuts deeply. All this time she has been the centre of my world, ingrained in every moment of my life, and now we finally meet again she doesn't even recognise me. Was I so insignificant to her? Everything we talked about? The time we spent together? Did it mean nothing to her? How can the same experiences have such a meaningful effect on one person and so meaningless an effect on another?

"Sophie…" I smile, stepping closer towards her.

"Get back," she says, her voice a high-pitched squeak. "Get away from me."

"I just want to talk to you." I move my hands down in a patting gesture and nod towards the sofa. "Let's go back through to the living room, sit down and have a chat, eh?" I'm trying to be the nice guy here, but she's not making it easy.

"No," she says, firmly. She's sidling across the room, back to the counter. If she darts, maybe she can get past me, but I'm almost certain I could bring her down. If I had to. It's not what I want. None of this is the way I wanted it.

"Stop!" I'm less relaxed than I intended. I'm not in control of the situation, or of myself, and I can feel my blood pressure rising. I have to keep myself in hand. I can't get carried away now. This is too important to mess up. If I don't chill, bad things could happen. Awfully bad things.

She shakes her head again and moves backwards slightly, almost tripping against the cupboard. "Get out of here. I'll phone the police. I'll…"

"Your phone is on the table there," I point through to the living room. It's closer to me than it is to her. She's made a basic error coming into the kitchen. I don't know what she was thinking.

"You won't be needing it. Everything is fine here, Sophie. We are fine, aren't we?"

I'm trying to be reassuring, but it doesn't seem to be having the desired effect. She's getting more panicked, her eyes are wildly searching for something to help her, and it seems obvious she's trying to concoct a plan.

"What do you want? Money? I don't have any money. Really, I don't. Not in the house, not in the bank. I have nothing. My husband disappeared and left me with a huge mortgage and... why am I telling you this? I don't have anything, okay?"

She has enough to pay for psychiatric care, so I know she's lying, but it's not money I'm after of course. It's time with her. It's words. It's the truth. There are a lot of things I want, but none of them are related to money.

Perhaps I should have kept hold of my own truths for a little longer, but I can't help myself. The words come out before I can stop them.

"It should have been me. Jack didn't deserve the grant. He didn't deserve to be chosen for Arkhangelsk. He never deserved you."

"Who *are* you?" Her voice is fragile. She's already given up. The feisty impression she's trying to show is all front. Those words still hit me like a punch.

"You don't even know who I am? You don't remember me?"

Now she does stop. She scans my face, looking me over. I've seen her every week, and she doesn't recall seeing me at all.

"You don't even know who I am?" My words turn into a screech as I repeat them, and I hate the way they ring around the room. "You pass me in the street, you walk by me in the Kwik Shop, and you never notice me. I make sure of that, yes, but think. Think back further."

Sophie backs up, and she's as close as she can be to the counter now. There's nowhere left for her to go. I can see her reaching, wafting her hand around for… for what? A knife, probably. Something, anything she can lash out at me with. Her

244

hand meets only air, and then the edge of the chopping board, but we both know that's not going to help her.

"Stop, Sophie. There's no point trying to fight me. What are you going to do, hmm? What do you think you're going to do?"

"Oh my…" And there it is, the first stirring of recognition. "I… I know you. I *know* you. Where do I…?" There's no space for her to back further away, so she bangs her buttocks against the cupboard door, her hip smacking into the handle.

"No," she yelps. "I know you."

"Then say my name. Who am I?"

"I…"

"You don't even know that, do you?"

"I'm sorry. I…" I can almost hear her thoughts as she looks around for options, scans for a way out.

"This should have been my life. I worked harder than Jack. I crawled my way up through the ranks for longer than Jack." I can't hold back the words. It's time she knew. "I loved you more than Jack... love... love you more."

"W-what?" she stammers. "Love? What?" She wobbles and reaches towards the counter once more, this time to steady herself.

"Of course, you never knew. You were so wrapped up in him, you couldn't see anything else. But if he loved you, Sophie, why did he go away? Why did he always go away? If you were mine, I could have let everything else pass me by. I wouldn't have needed to chase the major expeditions. I would have stayed here with you, building our life here. I wouldn't have gone to America, to Australia, to damned Arkhangelsk. I would have been with you. That was all I wanted. But he had you and he wanted all of those places, too. Nothing was ever enough for him."

Her confusion is cracking. "You wanted to go to Russia? But why?" And again, more calmly now, she asks, "Who are you?"

"I was part of the team for four years before Jack arrived. I was with Serena for seven years before she met Jack. He wanted everything I had, and piece by piece, he took it from me. It didn't matter to him that he already had you. He had a perfect life all along, but he couldn't see it. He didn't want it. He didn't want you."

I can't help myself. The words gush out of me.

"There's something wrong with the whole human race. All we want are other people's lives. Even if we have everything we need, it's not enough."

Take a breath. Calm down.

Sophie's expression is a combination of confusion and fear. Confused is understandable, but I don't want her to be scared of me.

"I know what he put you through. I understand why you did it," I say. Finally, she is within arm's reach, and I move towards her. Too quickly though. She darts away and raises her voice.

"Stay back. Keep away from me. I'll scream. I'll…"

"You won't scream. I know too much, Sophie. You don't want to go upsetting me. Not now. Not ever. How about the two of us go through to your lovely little lounge, take a seat, and talk this through?" She didn't take up the offer the first time, but now, she looks through into the other room as if considering the invitation.

She doesn't have much of a choice.

With a heaving sigh of reluctance, she lets me guide her through to the lounge.

The room bears little evidence of Jack ever having lived here, and I can't help but wonder if it was like this when he was still here. The bookshelves are filled with Plath, Dickenson and other such nonsense and I can't believe the dotted jars of scented candles were his choosing. Sophie has curled her tendrils around this room like Japanese knotweed, infiltrating and invading every nook.

When we live together, there are going to be some changes.

I'm so busy taking in the decor that I almost let her grab her phone. I scoop it up in time and stick it into my pocket.

"Hey," I snap. "Don't get any ideas."

"Why are you doing this?" she asks.

"Sit," I say, pointing towards her own sofa, as though she were the guest and I the homeowner. In another world, this would have been my home. Sophie and I could have lived here together long before now. Once we have cleared up the Jack-shaped mess in our lives, we can start afresh.

When we are both sitting, her on the settee and I on one of the armchairs, I reply to her question.

"I had to keep an eye on you," I tell her. "Make sure nothing happened to you. Make sure you were safe."

"You were watching me? The whole time? It was you?"

I want to interrupt her, but I'm polite enough to let her speak.

"I thought I was losing my mind, seeing ghosts. I *knew* someone was following me. I'm in *therapy*." I know she must be upset when she comes out with that. It's not like her to casually mention her sessions. "Do you not understand what this is doing to me? And now what, what do you want?"

"I have been watching you, but not in the way you think. You know, it was quite a serendipitous turn of events when you started visiting dear Doctor Thacker. Those two women he works with are so wrapped up in other people's lives, gossiping and sniping, that it was so easy for me to get past them."

She's sitting with her hands on her lap in front of her, in that good old defensive pose. I think for a second that I should go and sit next to her, take her hand, be gentle and tender in the way I've always dreamed of.

But I don't.

"I don't understand any of this. How have you been watching me? I never saw you. You followed me there? And then what?"

"It was pure chance that I found out about your appointments. I was behind you in the shop, you were on your phone, talking to Henny or Lola, whoever's turn it was that day."

I forgot for a moment that wasn't their real names, but I don't have time to explain everything to Sophie right now. I have my own confession to make.

"When I saw you go to Thacker's, I made a visit to the clinic, too. I planned a disturbance in the waiting room that would distract the staff while I was in the psychiatrist's office. That got Thacker and those two useless women to leave me just long enough to set up two snazzy little surveillance devices. Not the most high-tech of systems, but they've done the job. The cameras are much more effective than your doorbell monitor there. I've watched every one of your sessions. I've heard everything you've said."

"Why would you do this? What's the point in any of it? What did you think you were going to achieve?"

She has so many questions, but I let them run, because soon I will have questions for her. And I'm going to get answers. I smile as genuinely as I can manage and try to explain.

"I wanted to get to know you, the real you. I wanted to listen to your thoughts and your fears. I wanted to be on your side. Because Sophie, I think you need someone to have your back. If anyone found out what happened to Jack, well, you might find yourself in need of some help."

The fear in her eyes doesn't subside, but it changes in nature.

"What?" The word is so quiet I can barely hear it.

"You heard me, Sophie. Did you never stop to wonder just how long I've been watching you? I didn't see what you did to Jack, but I know his disappearance was down to you."

She rocks slightly, and I'm glad I got her to sit down before we had this conversation. If she had fallen on that cold slate floor in the kitchen, I don't know what would have happened to her.

"You don't know anything," she says, as though the colour has drained not just from her face, but from her voice.

"I don't know everything, but I know too much. I know enough."

Her words dry up, and she looks at me with an expression that I can't quite decipher.

"I know you," she says.

Then she mutters the one word I've been waiting to hear. She doesn't look up and speak it to me directly, it's tossed out as though it means nothing to her. She speaks my name.

CHAPTER THIRTY-ONE

Sophie's realisation of who I am wasn't quite the high point I had imagined, when I tossed this situation over in my head. For all those months, I've imagined her walking towards me, smiling, speaking my name as though I'm her saviour. Instead, I got a throwaway mumble.

She's confused, I tell myself. She doesn't know any better. She knows your name, but she doesn't know who you are, or what you're prepared to do for her. I hold back, and instead of leaping over, sitting with my face inches from hers and asking her what the hell she thinks she's doing, disrespecting me like this... instead I count to five, silently in my head, focussing on each syllable of every number.

I'm so wrapped up in the knife-edge situation that I don't hear the intruding sound at first. My whole body is poised like a cat, waiting to pounce, my muscles tightly coiled, ready to spring. When Sophie looks over in the direction of the door, though, everything snaps into focus.

There's someone ringing the doorbell. That loud, artificial sound I could hear from outside even when the door was closed is blaring all around us. It's almost unbelievable that I didn't notice it, but I guess adrenaline gives you blinkered vision, or whatever the auditory version of that is.

"Are you expecting someone?"

I search her face for clues. I need to know she's telling the truth this time. For once.

"No," she says. Her voice is unbelievably emotionless, despite the situation she's got herself into. I know she must be bluffing.

"Don't do anything stupid," I say, and as the words come out of my mouth, I realise I sound like every antagonist in every crime thriller I've ever seen. But if anyone thinks that's what I am, they're wrong.

I don't want to have to put my hand over her face. That can't be the first time I touch her. I didn't want it to be like this, but from that first meeting, could it have been any other way?

She was Jack's wife; I was in a long-term relationship with Serena. Neither of us were looking for anything or anyone else. Then again, I didn't think Serena was either. It's not just adrenaline that gives you blinkers.

That's not the point.

That's not what I want to think about right now.

When I first met Sophie, I knew she was special. It's heart-breaking, absolutely soul destroying that she doesn't even remember me.

"Alright? Nothing stupid." I tell her again.

She shakes her head, exaggerating her obedience, and when the doorbell rings for a second time, she fixes her eyes firmly on mine.

"We'll wait for them to leave, shall we?"

Sophie nods her head rapidly. It's reassuring that we are on the same page. She doesn't want trouble any more than I do. We think the same way, we see life the same way. I was right all along. We are meant to be together.

A few seconds pass after the last ringing before whoever's out there starts banging on the door.

I can't hide my accusatory look in time. I knew she was lying. Sophie, Sophie, why do you do this?

"You *are* expecting someone." My voice is a reedy whine, and I hate it. It seems I can't hide anything anymore. How is she ever going to respect me when I talk like this?

"No, I…" she begins, but then a look of recognition sneaks its way onto her face. She didn't know before, but she has just realised who's outside.

"Thacker?" Did he try to phone her? Is he more competent than I thought? Would he really come straight over here?

I stand up and move over to Sophie. How threatening can I be without ruining everything?

257

I can see from her expression that I'm wrong. It's not the doctor. Sophie dips her brow in a short sharp squint, like she just uncovered an interesting thought, and just as quickly straightens her face.

Would Thacker have called the police?

If he's worried there might be a risk or harm to the patient or to others...

What risk is there in telling him that another patient's husband didn't go on a work trip?

The banging isn't letting up. I look around for the video screen, trying not to take my eyes off Sophie for any longer than I have to. It's on the wall, next to the thermostat.

"Okay." I motion for her to stand up, move over to the monitor. We can at least see who's out there.

As soon as we get close enough, I can make out a figure, and immediately I know who it is. I can't quite get my head around who I see. If Thacker was confused about one of his patients knowing about another, that's nothing compared to how I feel when I see the figure on the doorstep.

Tall, blonde, slim. Unmistakable.

It's Serena.

CHAPTER THIRTY-TWO

Jack.

I'm putting on a show of trying to get my life back to normal, but I know it can never be *normal* again. Not until I face what happened.

I have to make peace with what I've done. I need to talk to Jane. I need to start calling her by her real name, I suppose. That might be a starting point.

Facing what happened means finding a way out of this. I'm always going to feel like I'm in danger until I can work out how to end it. I see people watching me everywhere I go because I'm terrified there's somebody that knows what I did. I can't go on like this.

It ends how it began: with you and Jane. The two of you together.

Jane. Plain Jane, we both called her. That's how you referred to her when you started working together, and after I met her at that party, I wanted to keep up the illusion to make myself feel better about you and her spending every day in each other's company. After a while, it stuck, and I almost forgot her real name.

I knew there was some kind of spark there, even back then. Right at the beginning I had one of my gut feelings, and I should have believed it. Perhaps I'm the one that's to blame for not trusting myself.

When Serena got back from Russia and phoned to say she wanted to come over I almost answered with a very rude "who?".

Serena.

We never used her real name; it sounded like a foreign language.

I let her come over because I was playing the role of bereaved wife. Or at least that was the primary reason. I let her come over because she was the only other person who really knew you. I wanted someone to talk to, someone who understood, even if it was someone that you had betrayed me with.

Now, I need more from her.

You'd be horrified, I'm sure, to think of the two of us talking about you. But you have to understand, she's all I have left of you now. I have to try to comprehend what happened - what happened between you and her, and what happened to us – because I don't know what to do next. Looking backwards is my only hope of figuring it out.

I didn't plan out an endgame, so I am lost.

Whatever happens next, I'm ready for this to be over.

S.

CHAPTER THIRTY-THREE

I have to act quickly, but I need time to think. Serena isn't going away; I can tell that much. I'm not sure how I'm going to play this, but there don't seem to be any alternatives for the first step. If she's not going away, we have to let her come in.

"Looks like we're having some company," I tell Sophie. "Act naturally. Behave yourself, okay?"

I nod towards the monitor.

Sophie's round-eyed expression is so calm that it unnerves me. She should be terrified, but instead, she appears almost apathetic. Has she given up? Is it the antipsychotics? I pause in my tracks to stare at her for a moment before carrying on.

"Go on. Open it." I say. I almost grab her and push her in the right direction, but I hold myself back. I can't treat her like that. She deserves better. "I don't have to tell you, do I, not to do anything stupid? This doesn't have to end badly," I say. "For anyone."

I don't want to do anything stupid either. This is so far away from how I wanted this to play out.

Sophie opens her mouth as if to say something. I think she's going to ask what the hell she's meant to say to our visitor, but instead she thinks better of it. Good girl. Letting out a small, defeated sigh, she walks to the panel on the wall and picks up the handset.

"Sorry," she says in a light, chirpy voice that sounds dangerously genuine. "I was out back. Come in, it's open."

I don't want our visitor to see me straight away.

I whisper in Sophie's ear as she presses the entry button.

"Sit down and play nicely. Don't…"

"I know. I won't."

This time I believe her. She knows what's at stake here.

I tuck myself to the side of the kitchen door, where I can just about manage to see Sophie, and our new guest, Serena. My past and my future, there together. This is surreal. I can't quite believe it's happening.

When Serena walks into the house, I can tell from her expression she's been here before. There's none of the looking around, taking in a new environment that she would have if this were her first time. I can't help but wonder if she came here to meet Sophie, or whether, prior to that, she came with Jack. Now isn't the time for me to let my thoughts meander down that route. Thinking about Serena and Jack together, and what he did to my life can't make the situation any better here, and will more than likely make it worse.

Serena is dressed well for the occasion, or at least she would be if the occasion were coffee at your ex-lover's wife's house. Is there a name for a female cuckold? If so, I suppose that's what Sophie is. What does that make me? She looks as though she has chosen her clothes to set herself apart from Sophie: sleek cream trousers, a green leaf-pattern silk shirt and cute kitten heel shoes I've never seen before. Time has passed, she has moved on, and her new wardrobe reflects the changes she's made. It's been less than a year since she left me, and I'm already wondering whether she is the same person.

While I'm wasting time taking in Serena's wardrobe choices, I'm not thinking about what I'm doing here, or what she's doing here, for that matter. Sophie has, true to her word, sat Serena down on the sofa, and I hear her offering a drink to our guest.

"It's too early for a wine, I suppose," Serena says, with that edge of a smile in her voice that I know means she is only half-joking.

"Perhaps a little," Sophie replies. "I've got a pot of coffee in the kitchen if you'd like one?"

That causes me to frown. There's no coffee pot here. The surfaces are clear, and everything is clean and neat. I could live here. I could live like this.

I've let myself become distracted again, and I'm caught off-guard when Sophie walks through back into the kitchen.

"What now?" she asks in a whisper. Her tone makes it sound as though we are co-conspirators, rather than that I have come here uninvited to ask difficult questions about her missing husband. I have to take control. I've got to get back on top of the situation, focus and guide us onwards.

"Let's go and talk to our guest," I say, as though it's the most obvious suggestion.

Sophie sniffs out a tiny laugh of disbelief. "Our guest?" she asks, but doesn't wait for an answer. "If that's how you want to play it, okay."

Before I can pull her up on her attitude, she walks back into the other room and sits down on the armchair. Clearly, she wants me to be as uncomfortable as possible when I come in and have to sit next to Serena.

"Did you forget the coffee?" Serena asks with a polite smile.

"I'm not sure you're going to be wanting that," Sophie says. Her voice is too confident. Does she think that Serena is going to side with her? Are the two of them going to plot against me? No. Sophie isn't like that. I can't let myself believe it.

I've got to think on my feet but when I do that, I tend to get things wrong. I'm not going to let Sophie be the one in control here. This is my showdown, not hers. I'm going to get her to tell the truth, and then, and only then, we can move forward. Together.

How Serena is going to fit in with that is anyone's guess.

Bracing myself, I step through into the living room. Sophie has her back to me, but Serena is face-on to my entrance.

"What the...? What are *you* doing here?" The visible surprise on Serena's face is almost identical to the look she had when I confronted her about her relationship with Jack all those months ago.

I ignore the question and try to ignore my thoughts.

"Isn't this a cosy little get together?" I say. I can't disguise the sneer in my voice. I don't want to sound like the typical villain, but everything is happening too quickly. It's out of my control. This isn't how I planned this meeting to go, and now everything is ruined.

Poor Serena. She and Sophie are very much alike, in so many ways. In another lifetime, the two of them could have been good friends. The kind that sit around the house drinking wine and watching rom coms while their husbands are away on trips abroad. Jack and I could have been friends too. We once were, but in an environment where there are limited resources, it's impossible for two alphas to exist in one pack. He applied for the missions I wanted. He wanted the woman I had. He got everything.

And now he is gone.

CHAPTER THIRTY-FOUR

Serena looks from me to Sophie, and I can almost hear her brain ticking away, trying to work out what's happening.

"Quite the reunion, isn't it?" I say. "Although it seems like we are missing somebody."

I have more questions than dear Doctor Thacker. I've heard him asking so many over the past few weeks. Asking Sophie, asking me. I only started going to those sessions because I wanted to know what it felt like. I wanted to experience what Sophie was experiencing. What a wonderful job it must be to spend your days listening to other people's lies.

Sophie's muscles tense, and I know I've hit a nerve. She's the biggest liar of the three of us. Sweet little Serena had her fun with Jack, but when it all came out, at least she didn't try to deny it. Neither of them did, but concealing the truth is the same as lying.

And me? I've been watching Sophie every week at her sessions, sure. I lied to the staff at the clinic, cleared Doctor Thacker out of the room just long enough to pin up the two surveillance devices. They were nothing special, but they've done their job.

I never intended to spy on her sessions. I would much rather have watched her at home. All that extra time I could have had observing her little life, but no. Jack had made this place into a fortress. No good to her now though. Once you let someone into a fortress, you're stuck with the problem of how you are going to get out. And here we are.

"What's going on?" Serena asks, her voice wavering.

"Serena. I know you are an intelligent woman. Much as I hate to admit it, I know you cared about Jack…"

"Please. Don't start…"

I wave away her interruption and carry on.

"I know you cared about Jack. You told me that it was all over between you before he disappeared, but you must have wondered what happened to him." I take a quick look at Sophie and then turn to Serena for a response.

Despite having no idea what's happening, she's sitting compliantly, making no indication that she's about to leave. Good. That's good at least.

"Of course," she says. "Sophie. I don't know if this is any of my business. I only came over to try to give you some closure. I know how difficult it's been for you."

"You have no idea," Sophie says, unable to conceal the pain in her voice. I hate Serena for what she has done to her, for what she has done to both of us.

"Ladies, please," I cut in. "Now isn't the time for the two of you to air your differences. Serena,"

I say, turning back to my ex-lover, "I came here to help Sophie tell the truth about what happened to Jack. She's been seeing a psychiatrist, and I thought therapy was going to help. I though she would eventually tell him what she did." I shake my head and glance at Sophie. "But she just keeps lying."

"You don't know anything," Sophie says. Then she directs her attention to Serena. "I didn't do anything to Jack. I didn't."

Serena looks so confused by the situation, and I can't say I blame her. It's time we got to the point.

"I was going to come over and tell you that whatever you did, it doesn't matter, Sophie. I understand when you love someone, sometimes you have to do things that maybe other people wouldn't understand. But I understand. Jack was bad, and you had to get rid of him. It's okay."

Serena and Sophie look at each other, just a brief exchange, and it feels as though they are talking about me.

"He wasn't bad," Serena says.

"I wasn't talking to you," I say, as patiently as I can. "You had your chance with me, Serena, and there's no going back for us. I've been looking out for Sophie since Jack's been gone."

"Watching me." Sophie speaks quietly, as though she doesn't want to upset me, but her words are not meant kindly.

"Looking out for you," I repeat. "Watching over you."

"You were watching. Every session."

Serena raises a quizzical eyebrow, but I don't have time to explain to her.

"To be honest, Sophie, it's not like you said much. I wasn't trying to invade your privacy…"

"What?! How can you even think that way? You weren't invading my privacy when you were spying on me? Literally stalking me?"

"Not literally. Not at all."

"You *were* following me? Watching me every-where I went."

"I hate to break it to you, but I really wasn't. I set up some cameras, I watched your therapy sessions, but that's all."

"That's all?" Serena almost laughs. "Wow, don't you think that's enough? You were watching her? That's messed up. Don't you know how messed up it sounds?"

I raise a hand to silence Serena. "No. You don't understand. It wasn't like that. I was looking out for her. She needed…"

Sophie jumps in.

"If you want to look out for me, what are you doing here? What is this all about?"

Serena keeps quiet, and watches intently, looking from Sophie as she speaks over to me while I think of a response.

"I told Thacker the truth," I say. Might as well be honest here too.

"No, you can't have. You don't..." Sophie stops herself mid-sentence. "What truth? What did you tell him?"

"That Jack never went on that field trip. You told Thacker that he went to Arkhangelsk."

Serena frowns and looks at Sophie. "Why would you say that? Everyone knows he never showed. Isn't that what this is all about? He went missing, didn't turn up for the job."

"Yes, yes," Sophie says. She's in a tangle now though. I can see her eyes flickering, while she finds the right lie to tell this time. "I told the police that, of course. I never told them he went." Her eyes turn back to me. "I told only one person that Jack went to Russia - my psychiatrist."

"Thacker," I say, for Serena's benefit.

"Doctor Thacker, yes." Sophie says, and at least we can agree on something.

"So why...?" Serena asks a half-question.

"I suppose when I was trying to think everything through, it made sense to my brain to imagine he had actually gone. That he went missing doing what he loved." The words catch in her throat and she's on the edge of tears.

I open my mouth to speak, but Serena cuts in.

"What is the truth, Sophie? Do you know what happened to Jack?"

In one swift movement Sophie tries to get up from her chair. As soon as she starts to stand, I put my hand onto her arm. There's no thrill as I finally touch her skin. This isn't how I wanted it to be, but it's how things are. I've got to let it play out.

"Sit." My mouth is dry with disappointment. "You're not going anywhere." I half expect Serena to protest, but she doesn't. The two of us both want the same thing now – to hear what Sophie has to say.

Serena speaks more calmly than I could manage right now.

"Sophie. What did you do?"

278

CHAPTER THIRTY-FIVE

Sophie flops back down onto her seat, defeated.

"My husband disappeared," she says, with the emphasis on the word *'husband'*. "I told the police. They haven't found him. I don't know where he is. Okay? What do you want me to say?"

I'm about to speak, when Serena says exactly what is on my mind.

"You're lying."

"What?" Sophie says.

"You're lying," Serena repeats. "Oh my. Why did I never see this before? Why would he have disappeared? He had everything. He had just won a place on the most important trip we'd ever scheduled."

I want to cut in and say that I should have had that place, not Jack, but I bite my tongue and let her continue.

"And do you know what, Sophie? He was going to leave you. Just because he and I ended our affair didn't mean we didn't talk to each other anymore. We may have stopped being lovers, but we were still friends."

I don't want to hear any of this, but I think Sophie needs to, so I don't stop Serena.

"He was going to leave you," she repeats.

Sophie chokes back her tears, and says, quietly, "No. He wasn't. He wouldn't."

"Hey," I say. "Let's not do that."

But Serena's words seem to have been the catalyst we were searching for. Sophie rubs her eyes and speaks.

"If only the two of you could have been happy together, happy enough to not want anyone else, happy enough to not ruin my life, well..." She shrugs, as though it's no longer important to her.

"No point dwelling on that now. If you had made Serena happy," she says to me, "I wouldn't have..."

"What?" Serena's voice is getting louder with every word. "What did you do?"

Sophie leans forward towards Serena, but doesn't try to get up again. "You took him from me, and even when you threw him away again, he still wouldn't stay. I thought after having an affair he would at least feel like he had some sort of obligation to me."

"You wanted him to owe you something? That's a wonderful foundation for a relationship," Serena goads.

"I know that he didn't just disappear, Sophie. Let's put an end to this." Now I am the calm voice of reason. If we are playing good cop, bad cop, this is the role I prefer. I hate upsetting Sophie. All I have ever wanted to do is to unburden her of the past so we can have a happy future together.

Sophie puts her hands onto her face and rubs her eyes. Then, exhaling deeply, she starts to talk.

"I didn't plan what happened with Jack," she says. "It was an accident. You can't think I meant to…"

My expression has given away too much of my ignorance because she stops talking and instead shakes her head.

"No, no, no." she repeats. "You saw nothing. You don't know anything."

But it's too late. Serena and I look at each other, and that psychic communication is shared between the two of us this time.

"Sophie," Serena says. "What did you do?"

"The night before his flight. He had that champagne bottle in his hand. Waving it at me, as though him leaving was something to celebrate; like I was supposed to be happy." Sophie darts her eyes between us, as though looking for support. "How could he not see that getting what he wanted meant leaving me behind? Every time, in every way, that's what he did. His choices were selfish, all of them about him and what he wanted.

Work, women…" The glare she throws Serena is venomous. "He was a selfish, selfish man. All I ever wanted was for him to be with me. And to love me."

"Did you… Sophie, is Jack dead?" I ask the question, so Serena doesn't have to.

"Having you believe he's dead would be the easiest way for me. If there was a body in the ground, then that would be the end of it. Everything would be so neat and tidy. I wish I'd killed him." She stops in her tracks. "I didn't mean to say that. I don't mean it. I just don't know what to do."

Her wall of resistance has fallen. I can see it now. I can help her.

"Sophie. It's okay. I'm here for you." I don't go so far as to say *we are here for you*. I can't count on Serena yet. "I can only help if you tell me what happened."

"He's not dead," she says, weakly. "But he didn't disappear. I know where he is."

CHAPTER THIRTY-SIX

Jack.

The police said that you weren't officially missing. At first, that was a bonus. No awkward questions, no one to lie to.

But of course, you weren't in Arkhangelsk, and it wasn't going to be long until your team reported that little nugget in.

Your team. Serena and Caroline, out there at the station without you. Well, I'm sure that's not what Serena was hoping for. She would have much preferred if it were Caroline that didn't arrive. No real loss. Not that I know her, but I know Serena, or at least I know enough about her to make an educated guess.

I waited for the call, but when it finally came, the police officer was almost apologetic.

"We've contacted the base station," the officer's hollow voice told me down the phone. "And Jack never arrived in Russia. The driver waited at the airport for him, but he never showed."

I asked what they were going to do, whether they had any more leads to follow up, all the time hoping they would tell me the best thing for it was to wait to see if you came back. I didn't want to push it too far. I didn't want them to actually find you.

"I'm sorry, love."

"You're not going to do anything?" I tried to sound indignant without being too insistent.

"In most cases, the missing person has…"

They started to explain the same lines, in the same textbook way I had been told before.

"Chosen to disappear. Okay. I get it."

"If you think of anything that could help our enquiry…" the officer said, letting the suggestion trail off as though he didn't have time to finish the conversation.

"Sure. Yes."

That was the last thing I was going to do. How could I tell anyone where you were and what I had done?

The police had given up.

When I put the phone down, I poured myself a large glass of wine. There's no one to complain about my day drinking anymore.

I should have been ecstatic. No one was coming to look for you. I was in the clear, at least for a while. But I wasn't happy. I wasn't happy at all.

When everything happened, it was a spur-of-the-moment decision and I acted on impulse. I never thought about a long-term plan. How long can we go on the way things are? How can I live my life worrying every day that someone is going to find me out? Everyone is watching me. There's suspicion on every face I see.

And I don't see an end to it.

I can still hear your voice, saying those words: *"I have to leave you."*

I couldn't let you go. Not to Arkhangelsk. Not with her. You have to believe that I never meant what I did.

You were my love. From the moment we met, you were my everything. Before I found you, I was alone. I had nobody.

Even though you told me everything was over with Serena, I couldn't face the idea of the two of you there together, miles away from civilisation, thousands of miles away from me.

There was only one way I could think of to make sure you never went away again.

It makes sense when I explain it like this, doesn't it? I'm going to keep writing to you, even though I don't think I'll ever give you these letters. Perhaps when the dust settles, you can have them all.

For now, though, I'll say goodbye.

Sophie

CHAPTER THIRTY-SEVEN

The three of us sit in tense silence, Sophie looking at the floor, and the two of us watching her, waiting to hear her reply. This isn't one of those silences Thacker loves to sit through in the therapy sessions. If she doesn't speak soon, one of us is going to have to say something. As in the sessions though, I want the next move to be hers. I know she can do it. I know she can tell the truth.

"I stopped him from leaving me." Sophie's voice is quiet but serene now, as though she has come to terms with her words. "What else could I do? You have to believe me, though. I didn't plan it. It wasn't what I wanted. It happened. It just happened."

"Stopped him how?" Serena asks calmly, and it throws me off balance. She actually sounds intrigued rather than horrified.

It's almost as though they are discussing a cake recipe rather than the disappearance of their mutual ex-lover.

"It might be better if I show you," Sophie says. "I can take you to him."

"Can you call him? Bring him here? Where is he? Where has he gone?" Serena has so many questions, all of a sudden. I realise I'm sitting quietly, watching the two of them, trying to figure out exactly what Sophie has done.

Sophie waves away the interrogation.

"I can't call him, no. And he can't come here. I can take you to him though," she offers again. This time, she makes a slight nodding gesture towards the back door.

My brain starts to unravel why she would choose the back rather than the front as Serena continues with her questions.

"Did you hurt him? Is he alright?"

"He's fine," Sophie says. "Mostly fine."

"Are you going to say something?" Serena directs this question at me.

"Sophie. Where is Jack?"

I lift my eyes from her to beyond, over her shoulder, into the kitchen, to the back entrance. As the realisation hits me, I snap my gaze back to her.

"No…" I say. "He can't… all this time?"

Sophie wails a long mewling moan. "No!"

"You… how… why…?" I can't articulate my words. The answer to the million-dollar question was so obvious. Jack has been hidden in plain sight. He's been right here all along.

Something Sophie said in one of her sessions suddenly springs into my mind.

I spend a bit of time in the garden.

The thing about other people's lies is that sometimes, they aren't lies at all. Sometimes people find the truth too difficult to talk about, so they hide it within riddles.

"Serena, stay with Sophie," I say. "Don't let her out of your sight."

290

Serena flashes me a look that says *you don't tell me what to do*, but she nods.

"You think he's…" Rather than complete the question, she looks at Sophie, and the confirmation is clear in her broken expression.

"It's alright, Sophie," I say. "Everything is going to be alright."

"Sophie. Tell me you didn't…" Serena says.

"He's there," Sophie replies quietly. She fumbles in her pocket and throws a set of keys to me. "There are two locks," she says. "You'll work it out."

I don't know what state Jack is going to be in, I have no idea what I'm going to find out there, but I'm certain now that Jack has spent the last seven months imprisoned in his own garden shed.

The garden itself is surprisingly well cared for. I remember the weeds creeping at the front of the house, and can't help but notice the difference. She's not just been out here to visit her husband;

Sophie has put time and attention into maintaining this garden. I wonder how she has kept her focus on mowing the lawn and weeding the borders, knowing that her husband is locked up meters away. I'd love to convince myself these are the things we do for the ones we love, but as I walk down the path towards the shed, my faith in Sophie is wavering.

We can get back on track after this. There's still a way for us. She's still Sophie. I'm not so sure any of this is true anymore.

The shed itself is just as secure as the house. It's a concrete-built structure, and I assume it must be soundproofed, or Sophie's planless plan would never have held up all this time. There's a window on one side, but there's what look to be solid shutters on the interior, so I can't see in. I would have liked a glimpse of what I can expect before I get to the door. I can't imagine this is going to be a pretty scene.

The keys are heavy in my hand as I get to the door. There's a solid mortice lock by the handle, and a deadbolt near the top of the frame. These chunks of metal are all that are separating me from the truth, and are all that have kept Jack from his freedom. It seems absurd that such a small thing can make such an enormous difference to somebody's life. Not just Jack's life, but Sophie's too. Perhaps even mine and Serena's now.

Sophie's keyring only has five keys on it, and it's easy to work out which I need. Still, I fumble them in my nervous state of anticipation, and drop the bundle on the floor. The upcoming confrontation is not what I expected to happen today, but then this was never Sophie's plan either. I wonder how she expected that this would end. However it was, I don't think it was with her husband's ex-lover's ex-partner showing up to save the day. I hope she appreciates this when it's all over.

Finally, I slide the correct key into the lock, and unbolt the door. Then, I pause as I begin to unlock the mortice. This is my last chance to stop and consider any alternatives. I haven't given any thought to any other routes of action. Should I really open this door and face up to Jack? I don't want to do anything that might cause any trouble for Sophie. The police route is out of the question. It's not as though I can involve Thacker any further. The only way to end this is to start here. Unlock the door and set Sophie's future free.

CHAPTER THIRTY-EIGHT

For some reason I expected the interior of the shed to be dark, like some kind of prison cell. Instead, the warmth and light hit me as I cautiously open the door.

"Sophie?" comes a croaked voice from within.

I slip inside quickly, closing the door behind me and carefully pocketing the keys.

"No," I say. "Not this time."

A figure, sitting remarkably casually at a small wooden desk, looks up to face me.

"What the hell are *you* doing here?" he asks.

For someone that hasn't seen anyone other than their jailer wife for the past half a year, it's an unusual response. I might have expected some kind of plea for release, or gratitude at being discovered, but instead he looks at me quizzically, and it throws me off guard.

"I came to help Sophie," I say. "You look remarkably well. Considering."

Now Jack rises to his feet and flies across the room towards me. I should have been better prepared, brought a weapon or something. I didn't think it through. I can almost understand how Sophie felt when she first trapped Jack in here. I don't have time to think further, as his fist rises through the air.

"Don't," I say, grabbing hold of his wrist. Fortunately, he's too weak to actually hit me. Even before he was locked up in here, he would have been no match for me. Not that we would ever have come to blows before. No matter what he has done, what trouble he has caused me, I'm not a violent man.

Instead of trying to throw more punches, he sinks to the floor by my feet.

"You have to get me out of here," he says, his voice breaking into a sob. "She's crazy. She's kept me locked up for so long. Please help me."

This was more the kind of response that I was expecting. It seems normal that he would want me to help him to escape.

"Now, now," I say, patting him gently on the head. "Let's take a minute to have a chat first."

"Seriously?" he whines.

"I want to help everyone to come to a peaceful resolution here. I want this to end well. Don't you?"

He looks at me, searching my face to work out my intentions, and gestures his agreement.

"Sure."

The shed isn't all that small. I mean, compared to having the freedom of the outside world, it's tiny, but there's been room for him to walk about. He has a surprisingly neat desk, and a chair to sit at it. There's no bed, but Sophie has seemingly provided him with a sleeping bag and a comfortable looking pillow. The door at the other side of the room must lead to the bathroom, as it certainly can't be an exit. As far as prisons go, it's a decent space.

"It's a delightful place you have," I smile.

"Are you out of your mind?" Jack says.

"I do have some issues, as it turns out, but no. I'm not out of my mind." I have to be patient with him. He's been through a lot. "Let's talk about things?"

"How about you just let me out?"

I cock my head and try to remember all that I have learned from my sessions with Doctor Thacker. I want Jack to think about what he's done. Perhaps I can help him. Perhaps this can work out for the best.

"Why do you think Sophie locked you in here?" I ask.

"Because she's crazy." He stops, as though this is a decent answer. I remember that leaving the patient time to add more to their statements can be a useful technique, so I wait.

298

"Because she didn't want me to leave her. She couldn't handle not being with me."

He does understand then. He knows it wasn't her fault. She did it because she loved him.

"Why are you still in here though? It's been months. How have you let her keep you like this?"

It's an unkind question, but despite the situation Jack has found himself in, I still don't feel particularly charitable towards him.

"Do you not think I tried? The problem with wanting to keep people out is that it also works against you when you're stuck *in*."

I stand looking at him, not knowing what to say, not knowing what to do. Thacker would know. He would have the right words, the appropriate questions. I'm a man without a plan.

"Are you going to let me out now?"

His voice quavers. It didn't even cross my mind that I would eventually be doing anything other than opening the door and freeing him, but now we're here, face-to-face, and I'm the one with the keys, well, I'm starting to wonder if there's another way.

I lean back against the door and fold my arms before speaking.

"She's a beautiful woman, Sophie," I say, looking Jack dead in the eye.

"What? What are you saying?" The way he tightens his lips isn't exactly an act of agreement on his part, but I know he must see it too.

"You had the perfect woman, and you let her down for... for what? For someone that was already in a relationship? Okay, Serena and I had our problems…"

He moves towards me, and I gesture with my arm in a *stay-where-you-are* motion.

"We had our problems," I continue once he has stopped. "But you had no right to come between us. We could have worked it out. You could have been happy with Sophie. None of this would have happened."

"Shit," he says. "You think I deserve to have been locked up in this hole for however long it's been just because I screwed around? Look. I'm sorry I messed around with your girlfriend, okay. Do you not think I've had plenty of time in here to regret my decisions?"

"It's a shame," I say, "That you didn't think of all this before."

"I can't believe this," he stutters, shaking his head and teetering as though he's about to lose balance.

"Calm down now, Jack." I reach towards him, and he whips his arm away.

"Stay away from me you psycho," he barks.

"As I said, Jack, I have some difficulties, but I'm not a psychopath." He doesn't know the half of it, to be fair, but I've owned up to my wrong-doings, to Sophie, and to Serena. I have a clean conscience now.

I don't want to get it dirty.

"This isn't my fault," I tell him, lowering my voice, slowing down, trying to extract the bitter edge.

"Do you think it's my fault? Can you just let me out? I've been here for months. Months. I don't even know how long. I decided not to make marks on the wall every time I caught sight of the sunlight. It was depressing enough being here without keeping a record of it."

There must have been a way out. I can't stop thinking that, over and over, as I look around the room, trying to imagine what I would have done in the same situation. He can't have wanted to be out of here. He's safe in here. What good could it do to let him out?

As I'm about to give him the news he doesn't want to hear, there's a banging on the door. It looks as though I didn't need to have a plan after all. Sometimes situations have a way of working themselves out, whether you like it or not.

Jack and I share one last look, and I step away from the door just as it's thrown open. Jack's going to get his freedom after all. Sophie, on the other hand, might not be quite as lucky.

CHAPTER THIRTY-NINE

People don't get what they deserve in life. I've looked for so long at other people's lives and coveted what they have, but it never works out for me. Jack doesn't deserve to be let out of the shed. He took Serena away from me. He stopped me going to Arkhangelsk. He hurt Sophie in so many ways that even I can't understand them. I know that when the police officers bust open the door - a rather easier job once I had unlocked it – that he would have his freedom. He'll never have to pay for what he's done. I'll lose Sophie before she is even mine, and he, undeservedly, will continue to get everything he wants.

There aren't just a couple of police officers standing in Jack and Sophie's garden; there are a group of six, with two mean-looking dogs, perky-eyed and sharp-fanged. Whatever they were expecting to find here, they came prepared.

Beyond them, Sophie and Serena are standing side-by-side, just visible through the kitchen window, looking out at us. It's a surreal situation, the four of us together again like this. I don't have much time to reflect on it as the police guide bedraggled Jack and I into the house.

"Stay back, ladies," the officer to Jack's left says, as he escorts him onwards.

Sophie opens her mouth to say something, but thinks better of it. I notice though, and wonder what it was that she was going to say. Serena just watches, silent, one hand on Sophie's shoulder. Perhaps they could become friends after all. What were they talking about when I was out there with Jack?

When we get through to the living room, I realise that we aren't stopping there. The lead officer is opening the front door, ready to take us through.

"Hang on. I went out there to let him go," I say to the plump officer to my side. "I was saving him."

Those were my intentions. No need to tell these kind officers that I was thinking of changing my mind.

"You'll be able to tell us all about it at the station," he says.

I try to stop the forward motion, but as soon as I do there's a firm tug on both of my elbows to keep me moving on.

"But..." I look around, hoping to catch Sophie's eye. I don't want to implicate her. I can't tell them the truth about what happened here, but I need some help. She's not looking.

"Sophie? Serena?" I call.

Sophie doesn't show that she has heard me, and Serena doesn't reply. Instead, she pulls Sophie against her in a fake-friendly fake-supportive hug.

"Serena. Sophie. Please?"

"Keep moving, sir," my escort says.

"But I haven't done anything. I didn't..." I can't finish my sentence because Jack interrupts.

"It was him." Jack turns and points. "He did this to me."

"He's been watching me," Sophie says, breaking her silence now it suits her. "If you go to his house you'll find, uh, he was watching me. He had cameras set up at the therapist's office."

The convoy of people has stopped to hear this. Jack and I, and the officers surrounding us are crammed into the living room, standing awkwardly in a cluster, all ears on Sophie.

I almost laugh at the word she chooses to use instead of *psychiatrist*. Even now she doesn't want to admit that she needed help.

"He told me if I said anything he'd lock me up too. I'm so sorry. I know I should have, I should have said something, but I was scared for my life. I tried to get help. I told you there was someone watching everything I did. I didn't know how to get away from him."

307

Jack raises two fingers to his lips, kisses them and waves them in her direction, and right then, I know that this isn't going to lead anywhere good for me.

"You're Jonah Washington?" the officer asks me.

"No," I say, honestly.

"He's Nick Shelton. He worked with me. It's complicated," Jack says.

"He was my partner." Serena finally speaks, but not in my defence.

"Tell them I didn't do this." I'm sure she isn't going to let me take the blame for something I haven't done.

"He's a very disturbed man," Sophie adds, before Serena can say anything else.

"Ms…?"

"Serena," she says. "Serena Noble. I… I don't know what he's capable of." She stops, turning in towards Sophie and nuzzling her face against her shoulder in mock tears.

"You're the man who represented himself as Jonah Washington? We had a call from your psychiatrist," he says, giving the other officers a moment to take in the word. "He's very concerned about you."

"I only went to see him because of Sophie. I just wanted to see her..." I realise as soon as the words leave my lips that I shouldn't have said that. I'm opening a can of worms that I'm not going to be able to cram back in.

"So, you admit to having the surveillance equipment that Mrs Portman here describes?"

"No." I look from face to face, and all of them are looking at me. I know they are going to go to my flat. They'll search it and find everything they need to validate what Sophie is saying. There's no way I can hide it. "Yes. I was watching her. But it's not what you think. I wasn't..."

"He's crazy. Please, take him away." Sophie lets out a melodramatic wail. Sophie. My Sophie. The woman I have dreamed of being with for all these months.

It's as though the three of them are creating ad-lib drama, bouncing ideas off each other and going along with each other's lines.

"Sophie, why? What are you doing? Serena. You know I would never…"

"You wanted revenge," Serena spits. "You hated Jack because I left you for him."

The officers mumble in unison as she says this, but it's not even true. She didn't leave me for him. She kept seeing us both. She stayed with me right up until I found her out. Looking at the officers though, I don't think they want to hear my correction.

"No" is all I can say. "No, no, no."

"Keep moving, everyone. Let's go," says a gruff voice up front.

"No," I say again. "Sophie, please. Serena, stop this."

I get one last look at the two women, wrapped in a false embrace, unable to make eye contact with me, before two officers bundle me through the door and onto the path. The house doesn't look as attractive, and the neighbourhood doesn't look as desirable on the way out.

"Jack." I cry his name, but he shakes his head.

The officers help him into one vehicle while they shove me into another.

"I didn't do anything," I say. "I didn't do this."

All I ever wanted was for Sophie to be safe, and for her to be mine. I never imagined that the price for her safety was going to be my own freedom.

CHAPTER FORTY

Jack.

I've been writing to you for months, but I'll never show you those letters. This one, I will let you read, just once, before I burn it.

I'm sorry for what I did. I hope you believe me.

When you went out to get your equipment from the shed, I should never have followed you. I was panicking, I realise that now. My desperation to keep you from leaving took over my common sense. You picked up your pack and begging you not to leave me had no effect. I acted on impulse, pushing you in there and locking the doors. You know what happened, but I have to write it down to confess to you, and start to atone for what I have done.

There was never a plan. I couldn't think of a way to let you out, and I knew I couldn't keep you

312

in there forever. Going out to you every day, taking you food and water, it was like having a pet in a cage, and I couldn't bear to keep thinking of you like that.

You were my love, once. You are my husband still. Whatever you have done to me, I know you didn't deserve to be locked away.

Nick, on the other hand, does deserve it. He drove me out of my mind over the past months. He watched me, listening to my darkest secrets while I was in therapy.

When he went out to the shed to give you your freedom, Serena and I had the chance to talk. She told me about how he obsessed over her, and how he would watch her wherever she went. Nick knew that you and Serena were having an affair, and he watched you. He let it happen, can you believe that? He let it carry on until he couldn't bear it anymore and finally confronted Serena. Of course, she couldn't deny it, because he'd seen too much.

Nick Shelton is a dangerous man. He may not have been the one who locked you up in there, but he's guilty of enough that I have no shame in letting him take the fall for it. Serena agreed to go along with the plan. Out of love for you, or out of hatred for Nick, I don't know. I don't care.

All I know is that you are free, and I am free too.

And I'm sorry. I'm sorry for the past few months. I'm sorry for driving you away from me.

I think I should keep going to see Doctor Thacker, even though I'll never be able to tell him the truth.

Everything I did, I did for us. I did it to keep you.

People do strange things for love, and, Jack, I loved you.

Sophie

Dear Reader

Thank you for choosing to read Other People's Lives.

I hope you have enjoyed the book. If you liked it, please take a few minutes to leave a review on Goodreads, Amazon, or wherever you recommend books to others. Reviews help authors to find new readers and help readers to discover great books.

If you would like to read more of my books, please visit my website, jerowney.com where you can find links to all of my books. You can also sign up to my mailing list for a free novel and updates on all my future books.

Best wishes

J.E. Rowney

Made in the USA
Middletown, DE
22 February 2024

50170321R00187